The breath punched from her body. Blinking hard, she read it again. "Oh, God."

Luis *was* married.

Luis was married to *her*!

Her lungs cramped. She couldn't breathe.

"Head between your knees, Ruby." Luis gently supported her as he pushed her down to the bed and her head towards her knees. "Deep breaths. One...two... That's right. And again."

"I'm okay," she mumbled a few moments later, unsure whether to be relieved or not when he released her. Meeting his gaze, she suspected her agonized expression mirrored his.

"I'm sorry, Ruby."

"I'm pretty certain you didn't force me into this." She pushed the words through frozen lips and once again read the marriage certificate. The *legally binding* marriage certificate. That was definitely her signature.

Dear Reader,

Vegas weddings have always fascinated me. I can't help wondering why anyone would make such a huge and life-altering commitment so impulsively. How could that be a good idea? I'll admit it—I'm risk averse. That said, though, there's something incredibly adventurous and romantic about a Vegas wedding too.

After all, what if the person you've just met and married is your soulmate? What if nobody has ever made you feel so seen and known before? What if, just once in your life, you want to choose optimism and hope over common sense and logic? That'd justify taking the spontaneous plunge into matrimony, wouldn't it?

When Ruby and Luis wake up married, they're appalled, but their subconscious already knows what it takes them the rest of the story to discover—that they're soulmates who are meant to be together. It's the reason they want good things for each other; it's also the reason they agree to help each other out for the duration of the holidays by remaining married. And as we all know, there's nothing like a bit of Christmas magic to help a romance along. Especially when it's a white Christmas in the Swiss Alps.

Wishing you much love and joy this holiday season.

Hugs,

Michelle

Waking Up Married to the Billionaire

—

Michelle Douglas

Recycling programs
for this product may
not exist in your area.

ISBN-13: 978-1-335-59649-9

Waking Up Married to the Billionaire

Copyright © 2023 by Michelle Douglas

Harlequin Enterprises ULC
22 Adelaide St. West, 41st Floor
Toronto, Ontario M5H 4E3, Canada
www.Harlequin.com

Printed in U.S.A.

Michelle Douglas has been writing for Harlequin since 2007 and believes she has the best job in the world. She lives in a leafy suburb of Newcastle, on Australia's east coast, with her own romantic hero, a house full of dust and books, and an eclectic collection of '60s and '70s vinyl. She loves to hear from readers and can be contacted via her website, michelle-douglas.com.

Books by Michelle Douglas

Harlequin Romance

One Summer in Italy

Unbuttoning the Tuscan Tycoon
Cinderella's Secret Fling

Singapore Fling with the Millionaire
Secret Billionaire on Her Doorstep
Billionaire's Road Trip to Forever
Cinderella and the Brooding Billionaire
Escape with Her Greek Tycoon
Wedding Date in Malaysia
Reclusive Millionaire's Mistletoe Miracle

Visit the Author Profile page
at Harlequin.com for more titles.

To Helen Sibbritt, for her enthusiastic support of the romance genre and for loving romance novels as much as I do.

Praise for
Michelle Douglas

CHAPTER ONE

RUBY WAKEFIELD'S TEMPLES pounded and it took an effort to peel her tongue from the roof of her mouth. Dear God, what had she drunk last night?

Flashes of the previous evening flitted through her mind, slowly assembling themselves like the pieces of a jigsaw puzzle—an incomplete one, but it told her enough.

What hadn't she drunk?

It had been fun, though, and—

She froze, the *why* behind her wild night returning in a rush. Her hands and jaw clenched. Her stomach churned. The word *failure* sounded over and over in her mind. Yesterday afternoon, when the conference had ended, Howard and Hugh, the senior executives at her law firm, had taken her aside and told her she didn't have the *leadership skills* to be yet made a partner.

She'd been slogging her guts out for five years. *Five years!* She'd gone above and beyond, and they all knew it. She'd been expecting them to announce the partnership and then take her out on the town to wine and dine her—she'd thought that was what this entire trip to Vegas had been about. But apparently, not only *didn't* she have leadership skills, she had no work-life balance either. She buried her face in her pillow and fought the urge to scream. How on earth was one supposed to have a work-life balance when they were working towards a partnership?

We'll revisit our decision in a year or two.

Or two? Acid burned her throat.

Afterwards she'd met Luis in the hotel bar. Slowly her hands and jaw unclenched. Lovely Luis, who was staying in the same hotel, and whose business was concluded but who didn't seem in any hurry to return home to Switzerland. They'd taken to dining together, seeing a few of the sights, and comparing their impressions of Vegas—he some high-flying executive and she a lowly lawyer who worked for a stupidly horrible firm in Sydney.

Luis had taken her for a night on the town. *'We'll show them you're not all work and no play.'* They'd laughed, drunk cocktails, danced, downed tequila shots, thrown down an enormous amount of money at the blackjack table, drunk…champagne?

And they'd finally given into their desire for each other when they'd returned to her room. Five days of silently longing and aching, but holding back. They'd made love, and it had been…

A revelation.

She peeled open an eyelid. Luis still slept in the bed beside her. She closed her eye, a dreamy lassitude making her boneless. The lovemaking had blown her mind, and while they'd both had a lot to drink, it hadn't seemed to affect their, uh…stamina.

He stirred. She opened that eye again, watched as he opened both of his. A lazy smile flitted across his face when he saw her. 'Morning, sweet Ruby.'

She couldn't help smiling back. The smile became a grin. Apparently, the worst afternoon of her life had been followed by the most extraordinary night.

Grinning like an idiot, she rubbed a hand across her eyes, dying for a glass of water—dying to repeat the events of the night before. Flinching, she pulled her hand away as something scratched her eyebrow. 'Ow.'

Luis intercepted her hand as she reached up to touch a spot that smarted. 'Careful, you'll do yourself an injury.'

They saw the ring at the exact same moment— a huge fake-diamond dime-store ring. Her mouth formed a perfect O. So did his. Ooh, she'd forgotten about that. 'We had *a lot* to drink.'

His eyes danced. 'And you were determined to prove your leadership skills.'

She clapped a hand to her mouth. 'I *ordered* you to marry me.'

'And respecting your leadership skills as any sensible person should, I did.'

They stared at each other for a moment before dissolving into hiccupping fits of laughter.

It hadn't been a real wedding ceremony of course—just a fake one to give them the full Vegas experience. Grinning, she pulled the silly, glitzy ring from her finger. 'Tell me I can keep the ring.'

'You can keep the ring.'

She'd treasure it for ever, but it seemed silly to keep wearing it now. 'Luis, last night was wonderful. Such an adventure.' Sitting up against the pillows, and bringing the sheet with her in the interests of modesty, she stared at the ring. 'I don't have very many of those.'

Maybe her firm had a point about the work-life balance thing.

She wasn't going to keep working herself into the ground for nothing, though. If they didn't value her contribution enough to promote her, then...

Then what? an inner voice mocked. *You told your family you were going to be made partner this week.*

Oh, God! She had, and—

She slammed a lid on those thoughts. She wasn't ruining this moment with Luis thinking about her parents, Horrid Cousin Christa, or the fact that she was a failure.

Luis sat up too, took the ring and twirled it in

those rather magical fingers of his. 'Maybe it's time to start making time for some adventures, sweet Ruby.'

Oh, the way he said her name! It had her swooning.

One eyebrow hooked up. 'We both have another full day in Vegas…'

Another day to make memories that would lighten her life forever? *Yes, please!* 'What did you have in mind? I—'

She suddenly frowned.

He leaned towards her. 'What's the matter?'

The fingers of her right hand had found another ring—on the third finger of her left hand. She held it up for them both to see. 'I don't remember this.'

He stared at it, frowned.

She tugged at it. Oh, Lord, she couldn't get it off. She'd need soap and water for that, or hand cream. 'It feels real.'

He took her hand to survey the ring more closely. 'White gold,' he said with a nod.

'Are they…?'

'Diamonds,' he confirmed.

Set around the band were three flawless diamonds that sparkled in the morning light. 'Oh, God, Luis, please tell me I didn't rob a jewellery store. This is the most beautiful ring I've ever seen, but there's no way on God's green I could afford it.'

Fine nostrils flared. 'I seem to recall buying it for you. You thought it lovely and I…'

Oh, no, no, no.

'I keep the fake engagement ring, but you're getting this one back.'

'But I bought it for *you.*'

But even as he said the words, he threw the covers back to surge out of bed, his frown deepening.

The entire surface of Ruby's skin tightened, and logical thought fled. Her hand inched up to her throat as she stared at all the tanned, muscled flesh suddenly on display. Her breath jammed and she gave a funny little hiccup. Luis was quite simply the most beautiful man she'd ever seen— tall and lean with broad shoulders tapering to narrow hips and taut buttocks. Oh, God, she remembered digging her fingers into those in the throes of passion and—

Heat flared across her face when she realised she was gazing at him with the kind of hunger dieting women reserved for a plate of chocolate-glazed doughnuts. She tried to drag her gaze away but before she could, Luis turned back, holding aloft a folder.

His soft chuckle filled her ears when she covered her eyes. Through a gap in her fingers, though, she watched as he turned back around to pull on a pair of briefs before coming to sit on her side of the bed. 'Sweet Ruby, my nakedness embarrasses you?'

'Oh, I…' Heat flared in her face. 'I don't have a lot of experience with this kind of…'

'I know.'

Oh, God. Had her inexperience been so obvious? Had she disappointed—?

He bent down until their eyes were level and their breath mingled. 'Last night was wonderful. Don't think otherwise for even a second. But you told me you do not indulge in brief affairs. I was honoured you made an exception for me.'

Swallowing, she nodded, ordered herself not to touch him. One hand lifted to touch his cheek, completely disobeying her. 'You're an exceptional man, Luis. And last night was also truly exceptional.'

Firm, warm lips claimed hers, moving over them with an expert sensuality that had every sleepy nerve firing to life. Last night should've assuaged her greedy hunger, but she craved him again now with a bold need that would've mortified her if she'd been with anyone other than Luis. She kissed him back with a wild passion of her own.

Strong arms slid around her back, splaying there, each fingertip branding her with the fiery intensity of its owner and leaving her in no doubt of what he wanted. *Yes. Yes, please.* Her hands landed against his chest, relishing the muscled contours they found there, the solid strength of his neck, her fingers eventually burrowing in the thick softness of dark blond hair. With a bitten-off curse that sounded more like a caress, he dragged her into his lap. She straddled him as his hands caressed her breasts, his thumbs making lazy circles around her nipples as he pressed drugging kisses to her neck.

Unable to contain a moan, she pressed herself against him, neither the sheet nor the thin material of his briefs able to hide his erection. 'Luis,' she panted, begging, needy…on fire. Her hands danced along the muscled strength of his shoulders, tiptoed back down his chest to his stomach to—

Her eyes flew open when he gripped her fingers to halt their sensual journey. Breathing hard, he stared into her face, kissed her once more, with a fierceness that stole her breath, before setting her on the bed and retreating several feet away.

She swallowed. 'Luis?'

'I burn to make love with you again, but I need to tell you something first.'

A horrible thought shook her. They'd spent the last five days talking and sharing and enjoying each other's company, but… She backed up until she'd jammed herself against the bedhead. 'You're not married, are you?' She'd never once thought to ask.

He dragged a hand down his face.

Oh, God, he was! 'Turn around,' she choked out. He did as she bid, and she dragged on a T-shirt and her sleep-shorts—the nearest items of clothing to hand. She'd slept with a married man! How could she be so stupid? Her family were right. She'd never amount to anything. She was a screw-up, a failure, a disappointment.

'May I yet turn around?'

She tried to compose her features. 'Yes.'

He turned back slowly, as if afraid any sudden movement might send her scurrying for cover. He held the folder out to her. 'This is what you need to see.'

She was super careful not to touch him as she took it. She'd slept with another woman's husband. She'd never be able to meet her own eyes in a mirror again. She was the lowest of the low, the—

You didn't know.

What difference did that make? She should've checked, asked.

Pushing the thoughts away to deal with later, she opened the folder and read the single sheet inside. The breath punched from her body. Blinking hard, she read it again. 'Oh, God.'

Luis *was* married.

Luis was married to *her*!

Her lungs cramped. She couldn't breathe.

'Head between your knees, Ruby.' Luis gently supported her as he pushed her down to the bed and her head towards her knees. 'Deep breaths. One…two… That's right. And again.'

'I'm okay,' she mumbled a few moments later,

unsure whether to be relieved or not when he released her. Meeting his gaze, she suspected her agonised expression mirrored his.

'I'm sorry, Ruby.'

'I'm pretty certain you didn't force me into this.' She pushed the words from frozen lips and once again read the marriage certificate. The *legally binding* marriage certificate. That was definitely her signature. 'We did the fake marriage because it was…'

'A laugh.'

Neither of them was laughing now. Screwing up her face, she tried to piece it all together. 'Afterwards we ate ice creams and looked in jewellery stores at real engagement rings.'

'You fell in love with the wedding ring you're wearing.'

'It fitted perfectly.'

'And somehow that led us to think it'd be a fine thing to make our marriage real.'

'So we did.'

She pressed both hands to her face. 'Oh, Luis, I'm sorry.'

He hesitated then sat beside her, careful not to sit too close. 'We'd both had a lot to drink. It would be a simple thing to have this marriage annulled.'

She couldn't explain why, but her heart grew heavy at his words. 'Which is clearly what we have to do, because…well, it was madness.'

His whole body drooped. 'I do not know what we were thinking.'

She met his gaze once more, opened her mouth but he reached across, pressed a finger to her lips. 'No more apologies, sweet Ruby.'

He really ought to stop calling her that.

Frowning at him, she pulled in another breath. 'You aren't married to someone else too, are you?'

'I am not. You?'

She shook her head. Who'd want to marry a mess like her?

Luis, a traitorous voice whispered through her. Luis had wanted to marry her.

The reason for him calling a halt to their love-making, though, hit her now. 'Last night we were drunk and not making responsible decisions.'

'But this morning we're no longer drunk. If we were to make love now...'

They'd be tacitly consummating the marriage, *dammit*! Why couldn't they have remembered this real legal marriage later? *Much* later.

Her phone buzzed informing her that a message had hit her inbox. Leaping up, Luis gestured for her to check it while he moved across to grab waters from the minibar.

The message was from Christa. What on earth...? Christa only ever contacted her when she wanted something.

Hello everyone!

Oh, God. Even worse, this was a message to the combined family group.

I simply had to tell you the news before I burst. I've just been made Senior Liaison Officer with Crosbie and Larkin.

Crosbie and Larkin was the political consulting firm Christa worked for.

As you can imagine. I'm in absolute ecstasies.

A lump lodged in her throat. Christa had known—*she'd known*—that today was supposed to be Ruby's day. She'd deliberately stolen Ruby's thunder.

How wonderful it will be to celebrate both my and Ruby's promotions when she returns home from Vegas. Ooh, do hurry, Ruby, and put us out of our suspense. Did your firm make you partner?

Her eyes burned. It was as if Christa knew, and was doing all she could to rub salt into the still raw and bleeding wound that stretched through Ruby's psyche. Everything came so easy for Christa. Why couldn't she just once…?

What? an ugly voiced mocked. *Let you shine?*

As far as her family were concerned, she wasn't made of the kind of stuff that shone. Whatever it was that Ruby was made of, it was a bit tarnished around the edges.

'Ruby?'

It didn't matter what she did or how she did it, she'd never sparkle like golden girl Christa.

'Ruby?'

She crashed back, found herself blinking into brilliant blue eyes. Luis leant towards her.

'Bad news?'

She shook her head.

'That's not what it looks like,' he said, his voice so gentle it had a lump stretching her throat into a painful ache.

'Just a message from Christa,' she mumbled.

'Horrid Cousin Christa?'

She'd told him a bit about Christa the other night, shared how she felt as if she lived in Christa's shadow. She'd even confided to feeling as if maybe she was the one with the problem, that maybe she was paranoid. Bless him, though, he hadn't agreed.

'What is the mean cow gloating about now?'

His words startled a laugh from her. Lord, no wonder she'd married him.

Luis's heart clenched at the expression on Ruby's face, the disconsolate slope of her shoulders in her Tweety T-shirt with the matching soft shorts that were so baggy they practically reached her knees. They were in the softest butter-yellow cotton…and so thin it brought last night's memories flaring back to vivid life.

Which was the last thing he should be thinking of at this juncture. For pity's sake, he had woken up *married*!

And yet it didn't send panic racing through him, as he expected it to. Or, he suspected, as it ought. He still found himself fighting the desire to laugh.

And to make love with Ruby again. And then maybe just one more time after that. To fix it in his memory for good.

But…*married*?

His lips twisted. If only his mother could see him now. She'd be ecstatic. So would his father. Walter Keller always wanted Claudia Keller to have her heart's desire. And Claudia's current heart's desire was to see her son married. Whether he was happy about the arrangement or not.

Shaking the thought off, he focussed on Ruby again. 'What does Christa say?' He didn't like the sound of Ruby's glamorous cousin—anyone who made themselves feel big by making someone else feel small had a problem. Ruby was lovely. She didn't deserve to feel small.

'She's sent a group message to the family…'

He watched her throat bob as she swallowed and his hands clenched. 'Yes?'

'She's just been promoted at the firm where she works.' She glanced down at her phone, and the smile she tried to give pierced his heart. 'It's a big promotion. Comes with lots of responsibility, and a huge pay rise.'

He winced.

'And she simply can't wait until we can get together to celebrate our *joint* career successes.'

He bit back something rude and succinct. Ruby had been absolutely devastated when he'd met her in the bar yesterday afternoon. She'd worked so hard for the partnership, only to be denied it. And now Horrid Cousin Christa was gloating, clearly intent on rubbing Ruby's nose in it.

'I would give you a job that would trump hers in an instant!' He snapped his fingers with a growl. 'Just like that.'

She gave a half-hearted laugh. 'If I recall rightly, you made me that offer last night too.'

He had. And she'd turned him down. They lived on opposite sides of the world, blah-blah-blah. He couldn't give her a job when he barely knew her, blah-blah-blah. You couldn't offer someone a job when you were under the influence, blah-blah-blah. All reasonable points, but they didn't stop him from wanting to give her a job that would turn her gloating cousin an ugly shade of green. He and Ruby might've only known each other for five days, but he felt he knew her—really knew her.

Ruby thrust her phone face down on the bedside table. 'I'm sorry. We've far more important things to discuss than my stupid petty concerns.'

They weren't stupid. And they weren't petty. If only she would let him help—

He froze. Everything stilled.

If only…

Boom. Boom. Boom.

His heartbeat sounded loud in his ears and he slammed back into the moment, his pulse quickening and the razor-sharp business instincts that had made him ridiculously successful igniting.

If only she would let him help.

If only his mother could see him now…

He'd been searching for a solution. Could this…?

'Luis?' The touch of soft fingers on his arm snapped him back. He stared at Ruby, his heart pounding.

If only his mother could see him now.

She backed up a step. 'What?'

It could be a bad idea. He paced from one side of the room to the other. Or it could be inspired.

He'd been cooling his heels in Vegas, reluctant to return home to meet the parade of eligible women his mother had threatened him with these holidays. For reasons he'd yet to discover, it was suddenly of paramount importance he marry. Unbeknownst to him, some clock had run down and his time had run out. He hadn't even known a clock had been ticking!

Lifting his water to his mouth, he drank deeply.

There was no way he was marrying. His parents' marriage and subsequent divorce had proven to him that romantic love was a lie. He recalled their pain when their marriage had failed in all its ugly detail, their trauma—the guilt, confusion…the sense of inadequacy—and shook his head. He wanted no part of that.

He'd tried talking to his mother. He'd approached her on three separate occasions with the sole intention of finding out why it was suddenly so important to her that he settle down. She'd evaded him the first time—had murmured platitudes about wanting to see him happy, had said she was worried about him being lonely. He'd told her he was happy, had assured her he wasn't lonely. She'd waved that away with, 'That's not the same.' She'd then made some excuse about being late for a lunch with a business contact. She hadn't met his eyes once during the entire conversation.

The second time he'd asked her if she was ill, his stomach churning and fists clenching. Was *that* behind her desire to see him settled? She'd blinked and straightened and said absolutely not, holding his gaze the entire time. Glancing at her watch, she'd then feigned a yelp and raced off to some charity event. A lie. There hadn't been an event for that particular charity in the city that day. There hadn't been one for the entire week.

He'd checked. But her surprise that he might think her ill had been genuine enough.

The third time, he'd blocked the exit from the room, and demanded an honest answer. 'Why do you want to see me married?' She'd lost her temper. He could count on the fingers of one hand the number of times he'd seen her truly blow her top, and it had taken him off guard. She'd flung words like duty and responsibility at him like knives, had yelled that he owed it to her and his father. They'd given him every advantage in life, blah-blah-blah, and this was how he wanted to repay them? She called him hard-hearted, intractable, selfish…

He swallowed. She'd called him a disappointment. She'd never spoken to him like that before. Ever. It had left him reeling. When she'd brushed past him, he hadn't tried to stop her.

She hadn't apologised. She hadn't retracted the ugly words. She'd hadn't referred to the conversation again. But it now throbbed in all the spaces between them.

His father hadn't proven helpful. When approached, Walter had simply said, 'She is your mother. She wants to see you happy and settled. These are natural instincts, Luis. Is it really so much to ask?'

Apparently his happiness wasn't of any concern to either of them.

Resentment, though, had slowly evolved into

concern. Claudia Keller was an intelligent woman, usually level-headed. His hands clenched and un-clenched. He knew his happiness did matter to his parents. He knew it would hurt them to see him unhappy.

Something was going on, and he needed to find out what the hell it was. Instinct told him it was something serious. If she wouldn't talk to him… then he'd need to take more drastic action.

Squaring his shoulders, he turned back to Ruby. 'Ruby, it occurs to me that we could help each other out.'

She once again held that silly dime-store ring. When she realised he was watching, she dropped it beside her phone, and seized her bottle of water. 'I'd be happy to help you any way I can.' She lifted the bottle to her lips and took a long swal-low.

'If you were to stay married to me—'

She choked, water spraying everywhere. 'What on earth—?'

He waited for her coughing to subside before continuing. 'I believe I mentioned how my mother has been plaguing me to marry.'

She gave a wary nod. 'Apparently you owe it to her and your father, and you owe it to the fam-ily name to marry as soon as humanly possible.'

His hands clenched and unclenched. He had no intention of marrying to please his mother, but—

This marriage didn't count. They'd have it dissolved. But… Being married could buy him the time to find out what was going on, to find out why his being married mattered so much. Once he discovered the problem, he could fix it.

'You also know I haven't been in any hurry to return home.'

'Because you want to avoid your mother's matchmaking.' Her lips twitched. 'And avoid being introduced to a whole array of beautiful women, because, I mean, that would be a fate worse than death, right?'

He bit back a smile. *This* was why he'd spent so much time with Ruby over the past week. 'Ordinarily I'd agree with you, but I don't dally with women who are hoping for long-term commitment.'

He kept his gaze trained on her face, but she didn't pale at his words or appear suddenly disappointed. He let out a breath he hadn't been aware of holding. He and Ruby were on the same page. She hadn't been expecting love and commitment. He hadn't read her wrong. 'All of the lecturing would stop if I was married.'

Ruby took a careful drink, and then lowered herself back to the side of the bed. 'You're talking about remaining married for the duration of the holidays.'

'Yes.'

She nodded—not in agreement, but as if getting his proposition straight in her mind. 'I hate to point out the obvious, but as soon as we dissolved the marriage, the lecturing would start up again. This isn't a long-term solution.'

He paced again. It was a generous enough room, but nothing like his penthouse on the top floor. 'Not if we do it right.'

'Oh?'

'First, let me tell you what you will gain from the arrangement, because I don't expect you to do this from the goodness of your heart. As I said, we can help each other.'

She stared at him as if she were Alice and had just fallen down the rabbit hole.

'You and me, Ruby, we just want to live our lives on our own terms, yes?'

Her eyes flashed and she nodded.

'My family, they are a…big deal. The moment your firm hears of your connection to me, I can promise they will offer you the partnership you so desire, probably within a week.'

Her head came up and she didn't bother trying to hide her thirst for that partnership. Her need to prove herself made something inside him ache.

'Here is what you are going to do.' Walking across, he seized her phone and thrust it at her. 'You're going to call one of those partners right now, tell them that you're taking their criticisms on board, particularly the one about having no work-life balance, and that you're taking a month's leave, effective immediately, to have a long-overdue holiday and consider your options.'

He shook the phone at her until she took it, and then raised an eyebrow when she continued to simply stare at him. 'What are you waiting for?'

'You want me to threaten them?'

'This is not a threat. It is a negotiation.'

'And when they call my bluff and tell me they no longer think I'm a good fit for the firm, what do I say then?'

Her naiveté made him laugh. 'They will not want to lose you. You have let them make of you a slave. They expect you to now work even harder, so that this time next year you *will* make partner.' An event he had no doubt they'd keep delaying for as long as they possibly could. Ruby needed to develop a better strategy. And she needed to develop the backbone to see that strategy through.

She folded her arms, clearly miffed that he'd read her future so clearly.

'Imagine Christa's face when she realises you've been given the partnership?'

It was a cheap shot. But the more he considered his plan, the more he thought it would work.

'You really think me hinting that I'm prepared to walk away would have an impact?'

When combined with his family name, absolutely. 'It would take them a long time to find someone to replace you, and we both know time is money.'

She grimaced. 'That, at least, is true.'

'Furthermore, when they learn of your connection to me and my family, they will start to speculate how much business I might send your way.' That would seal the deal.

She chewed the inside of her cheek. 'You know how much I want the partnership. I mean, I've spent all week talking about it.'

It wasn't the only thing she'd talked about, though. She'd been interested in him and his life, in making him laugh and focus on the here and now rather than on the weight of expectations that had started to darken his life. She hadn't expected him to lighten her load or work any miracles. For heaven's sake, she had no clue who he was. Not really.

'And in return I spend the holidays with you and your family as your wife.'

'Yes.'

'And…? Because I sense there's an *and* or a *but* in there somewhere.'

She might not have much of a backbone, but she was smart, he'd give her that.

'I want my mother to regret putting so much pressure on me to marry.'

'How…?'

Her question was nothing more than a squeak, and a slow smile tugged at his lips. His plan was pure brilliance. 'Could you imagine my parents' horror at what they'd pressured me into, if I were to bring home the wife from hell?'

'You want them to *hate me*?'

'I want them to be appalled by you,' he corrected. Hate was far too strong a term. 'I want you to play the part of a gold-digging harpy. I want you to be the exact opposite of what my mother wants for me.'

Hopefully it would give his mother such a shock he'd be able to crack her until-now impenetrable armour to discover the deeper reasons that lay behind her demands.

She stared at him as if she couldn't believe what he was asking, and he rubbed fingers across his brow, finally locating the flaw in his plan. 'You, however, are a people-pleaser. This is a thing that you may not be able to manage.'

Her chin shot up. 'I can be as big a bitch as the next person.'

He seriously doubted that, but thankfully that wasn't what he wanted. 'I don't want you to be rude and spiteful or mean or anything like that.'

Relief flashed across her face.

'I just want you to be over-the-top impressed with the money. I want you to buy gaudy horrid things that will make my parents, who are the epitome of good taste, wince. I want you to nag me for a yacht and a holiday house on the French Riviera. I want you to ask what the rug in the breakfast room cost, and to ask their friends if they know how rich I am.'

She clapped a hand over her mouth, but the sudden laughter in her eyes had his blood fizzing.

'I want you to be totally and unashamedly...'

'Cheap and trashy.'

He'd been searching for less offensive descriptors, but he gave a nod. 'Yes.'

'And you really believe this will give you the space you need?'

'It will give me the chance to find out why this has become so important to my mother. Something is wrong and I want to fix it.'

Ruby had big hazel eyes—the green in the iris so very green, the brown a glowing amber—and they gentled now. He swallowed and rolled his shoulders. He'd never shared as much with anyone as he had with Ruby this week. They'd clicked, while both knowing their friendship had an end date. Would adding another three or four weeks to that end date be a mistake?

Surely not? As long as they were upfront and honest with each other, all would be fine. 'Ruby, I just want to fix whatever is broken and get life on an even keel once more. Do you think that's wrong?'

Reaching out, she squeezed his hand. 'I think it's admirable.'

He squeezed back. 'Thank you.'

She wrinkled her nose. 'While I just want to stop feeling like a failure.'

'Despite what your firm and your family make you think, you are not a failure. You're smart, you work hard, and you're fun. And in case you didn't know, that's a winning combination.'

She rubbed a hand across her chest, her eyes suspiciously bright. 'You really think this plan of yours will win me my partnership?'

'Yes.' Though why she wanted to continue working for a company who demonstrated such a lack of respect for her was beyond him. 'So... are you up for another adventure?'

She stared at him, moistened her lips. 'You said your family is a big deal. You're rich?'

He nodded.

'Are we talking *just* rich or crazy, over-the-top, extraordinarily rich?'

'The latter.'

'Oh, God! So the yacht and diamonds...? The house on the French Riviera...?'

'Could all be realities.'

She leaped up, and backed away from him. 'I'm not agreeing to this until we sign a prenup. God, Luis! I don't want your money. I just...'

'I trust you, Ruby.' And he did, surprisingly. 'And as we're already married, a prenup is out of the question.'

'We're signing a post-nup, then. This is non-negotiable. Your parents don't need to know about it, but I'm not staying married to you until you have protections in place for your money.'

What a remarkable woman she was. He held out his hand. 'Deal.'

CHAPTER TWO

RUBY STARED AT the hand Luis held out, and hesitated. 'There's one more thing.'

His hand lowered back to his side. 'Yes?' he prompted when the silence stretched too long.

She wanted to bury her face in a pillow.

'Ruby, you're a diligent employee, but you lack the leadership skills necessary to make partner.'

Squaring her shoulders, she forced her chin up. 'If we're going to do this…'

'And I really think we should.'

Oh, that voice… The accent. She wanted to close her eyes and bask in its warmth. The accompanying smile made her want to throw caution to the wind, and—

She swallowed, pulled back. She couldn't. She was adulting. She needed to prove that she *did* have leadership skills, that she had a backbone. She firmed her jaw. And if she could do that in her pjs, then she should be able to rock it in the boardroom. 'If we're going to do this, I think we ought to keep things platonic.'

His gaze flicked to the bed as if he couldn't help it.

Hold firm.

'Last night was amazing.' Eyes the glorious blue of a glacier—fresh, clean…sharp—moved back, and heat gathered in her veins. She ached to spend one more night with this man, but the stakes had suddenly climbed and she couldn't risk it all on a fling—no matter how extraordinary. 'But you don't want a real marriage.'

'This is correct.'

'You don't want any kind of a long-term commitment.'

'I do not.'

'You don't want to fall in love with me, and you don't want me falling in love with you.'

He stared at her for several long moments. 'I do not believe in love, Ruby.'

She blinked.

'But I understand that others do. I will not fall in love with you—this I promise. And if you were to fall in love with me, it would be a disaster.'

Wow, brutal. But honest. She appreciated the honesty. 'If we were to continue with the…lovemaking—' it was her gaze that drifted to the bed this time '—I'm worried I'd develop feelings for you. Feelings stronger than friendship.'

His jaw firmed. 'I see.'

His voice gave nothing away. Was he now having second thoughts? In that moment she knew she wanted to go ahead with his crazy scheme. She wanted that damn partnership!

The fact it would also mean avoiding a Christmas filled with Christa's gloating and her parents' long-suffering sighs and evident disappointment would be the proverbial cherry on the top of this figurative ice-cream sundae.

She planted her feet. 'As you say, if I were to develop feelings for you that would be a disaster—and uncomfortable for both of us.' Pressing her hands together, she pulled in a breath. 'You're lovely, you see.'

Something in his face softened. 'Ruby—'

'But I don't want to fall in love with you. I don't want that kind of heartache. But I also think you could become one of the best friends I've ever had.'

It hit her, all the things she'd sacrificed in her bid to make partner, and one of those things was friends. She'd sacrificed so much. She had to make it count.

Squaring everything—shoulders, jaw, fingers and toes—she hoped she looked fearless. 'We agree to a month-long platonic fake marriage—' that wasn't really fake but they'd deal with that later '—to win me my partnership and help you uncover your parental mystery.'

She held out her hand. Luis hesitated and she died a thousand deaths, until he too lifted his hand. They shook on it.

* * *

The nerves twisted in Ruby's stomach two days later as Luis drove his luxury sedan out of the airport and through the Zurich traffic, in the direction of his family home forty-five minutes away in the Canton of Glarus. Having travelled first class, they'd cleared customs in the blink of an eye. Her head was still spinning.

'Nervous?'

Luis's words made her start. 'What makes you say that?'

He raised an eyebrow though kept his eyes on the road. 'Ruby, you talked non-stop on the first and last legs of our flight—' they'd both napped during the middle leg '—but haven't uttered a single word since we left the airport.'

While they were still on the plane, their destination had felt a million miles away. Also, flying first class had been a brand-new experience, and there'd been so much to see, to experience, to gush about.

Then there'd been all the background material she'd had to gather. She'd quizzed him about where he lived, and, while he'd kept things low-key, she suspected it was all rather grand. She'd discovered that he was an only child, and that his divorced parents lived in separate wings of the same house. Walter and Claudia Keller had divorced seventeen years ago, but had apparently remained the best of friends. It all sounded terribly civilised.

She bit her thumbnail. If his family home had wings, it clearly was grand.

'What do you traditionally do at Christmas?' If his mother had planned to introduce Luis to lots of eligible women, did that mean there'd be lots of entertaining?

'It's usually pretty low-key. The three of us often travel for work so the Christmas week is usually reserved for having an actual break.' He sent her a look. 'Which is why I found it surprising that my mother wanted to entertain this year.' His face relaxed into a satisfied smile. 'My marriage to you, thankfully, will put an end to that nonsense, though.'

Excellent. The fewer people who thought her a gold-digging cow, the better.

'We do all the things that most families do, I suppose—trim the tree, go to carols by candlelight, stuff ourselves silly with too much food, and exchange gifts. With the ski slopes so near, and all of us avid skiers, we spend a lot of time on the slopes between Christmas and New Year.'

She grinned.

'What?'

'Your life is a fairy tale.'

One broad shoulder lifted. 'Except I am no fairy-tale prince searching for his princess.'

Except for that.

He glanced at her. 'I'm hoping this fairy-tale life of mine might provide you with some compensation for...'

Her stomach churned. 'Making your parents dislike me.'

'Disappointing them,' he corrected.

Horrifying them more like, but she didn't challenge him. Anyway, disappointing people was apparently her superpower. Just ask her parents. 'Despite what the senior executives of my firm think, I do have a backbone, Luis.' She could show initiative and make hard decisions.

He didn't say anything, and for the first time she wondered if maybe he agreed with her employers. She thrust out her chin. 'Leaders don't concern themselves with disappointing others if it's in the interests of the greater good.'

He raised an eyebrow.

'I believe you've every right to live your life the way you see fit. If marriage isn't for you, nobody ought to force the decision on you. Therefore, while I probably won't enjoy *disappointing* your parents, I support your end goal and *that* will keep me on task.'

'Thank you, Ruby.'

Her eyes narrowed. 'Are you laughing at me?'

'No.'

The quick smile he sent her was filled with so much warmth, her breath jammed, reminding her how powerfully attractive this man was. Patting her chest, she forced her gaze back to the view outside the car window.

'I think you're going to go home to Australia a changed woman. Your senior partners will hardly recognise you.'

She swung back. 'So you *do* think I lack leadership potential!'

'No, Ruby, I think you have enormous potential.'

'But?'

He hesitated. 'I think, perhaps, you've been chasing this partnership for so long that you have focussed on being what you think the partners want you to be rather than becoming your best self and developing your unique strengths.'

Her mouth opened, but words refused to push past the lump in her throat. With a superhuman effort she swallowed it. 'You make me sound like a martyr.'

That broad shoulder lifted again. 'I do not wish to offend you.'

He not only made her sound like a martyr, he thought her one too! 'I have a backbone.' She'd prove to everyone that she could be a success.

'This is what I mean when I say I think your senior partners will get a shock when you return to Australia. You are finding your strength and learning to use it.'

With a huff, she glared out through the windscreen. She would prove that she was a success.

'You are not offended, are you?'

Of course she was offended. He thought her a weakling. 'No.'

She thought he might challenge her, but instead he pointed up the hill to their left. 'There is my home.'

She turned to where he indicated. There was snow *everywhere*. And mountains. And it all looked breathtakingly beautiful. There was only one residence that she could see, though, and—

No way. 'Where?' She needed it clarified.

He pointed again.

Her jaw dropped. There was grand and then there was…*this.* 'That's not a house, Luis, it's a castle!'

'No, no, it is not fortified.'

'It has turrets!' Well, they were actually square towers, but each sported rounded windows…and there was at least one semicircle turrety thing halfway up this side of the building.

'It is rather beautiful, yes? We are proud of it. It is called Villa des Lufttals.'

Beautiful barely did it justice. Built of pale grey stone, the villa looked as if it had stood there for centuries. It probably had. At its four corners those square towers rose, their straight lines and curved windows utter perfection. She counted seven pale grey chimneys, all of different sizes, lifting above the red-tiled roof, but suspected there might be more on the side that was currently hidden from view.

As they drew closer, she saw that the building was neither symmetrical square nor rectangle, it was more haphazard than that with glimpses of courtyards and odd enclosed balconies dotted here and there, but somehow the alternate square-ness and roundness worked to create something breathtaking and harmonious.

'What do you think?'

'I think it's the most amazing place I've ever seen,' she breathed, pinching herself. 'I can't believe I get to spend the next month here.'

His smile widened and she nodded. 'This is definitely one of those compensations you mentioned.' Not that she needed any of those, but it didn't mean she couldn't enjoy them when they came her way. She'd prove to him that she had a backbone, and then she'd return to Australia and prove the same to her firm.

'Seriously, though, if I were your lawyer, Luis, I would haul you over the coals for making such a reckless marriage. I could've taken you for such a ride.'

'But you didn't, and you won't.'

He was darn tooting she wouldn't. Especially now they had a nuptial agreement in place. She was entitled to precisely diddly squat, and that was as it should be. She pressed her hands together. 'Please promise me you will never marry so rashly again.'

His lips tightened. 'You have my word.'

Why was he so against marriage? If they weren't about to meet his parents, she'd ask him.

'Don't forget, though. I *want* my parents worried that you might be the kind of girl to take me to the cleaners.'

She mimed zipping her mouth, nerves jangling through her again. She did her best to ignore them. She'd do all she could to help Luis get his nagging mother off his back.

The expression on his face when he'd confided having to constantly parry his mother's manoeuvres, the way his shoulders had sagged and eyes closed… It caught at her again now. She'd sensed his bewilderment. And his hurt. She understood both of those emotions when it came to family.

How could his mother be so unreasonable? So *unkind*? Why couldn't she love Luis for who he was rather than what she wanted him to be?

He'd said he suspected something was wrong and that he wanted to find out what it was so he could make it right. He had such a big heart. And she planned to do everything she could to help him.

Staring at the fairy-tale residence in front of her, she imagined Claudia and Walter Keller as straightlaced and cheerless, with *very* rigid ideas about what constituted good breeding. Duty would be a word they'd no doubt bandy around like a weapon. *Bullies.*

She *would* remain firm. Still… 'Are they going to yell at us when they discover we're married?'

'I shouldn't think so.' He glanced at her. 'Are you frightened?'

'Absolutely not.' She straightened. 'I'd just like to know what to expect.'

'If it's any consolation, this is as new to me as it is to you.'

'Never mind, I'll hold your hand,' she teased, wanting to lighten the sombreness that darkened his face. 'And don't forget that while we have a job to do this coming month, it doesn't mean we can't have fun too.'

His eyes lightened. 'My poor parents aren't going to know what hit them.'

He manoeuvred the car through a set of enormous gates, along a wide tree-lined avenue, and drove around to the back of the villa to park in an enormous courtyard. 'Stay there,' he ordered, coming around to open her door. Holding out his hand, he said, 'Ready?'

He had enough to deal with, she wasn't going to let him worry about her too. Placing her hand in his, she grinned up at him. 'You bet.'

The door swung open before they reached it, and beside him Ruby stiffened. '*Hallo*, George,' Luis called out, to let her know it wasn't his father. He should've told her his parents would both be at work. She wouldn't meet them until this evening.

'*Guten tag*, Luis.'

Ruby's elbow dug into his ribs. 'You have a butler?'

He raised a deliberately supercilious eyebrow, but he suspected his grin ruined the effect. 'Of course. It takes a veritable army to maintain a place of this size. George, this is Ruby.'

'*Guten tag*, Miss…?'

'Just Ruby,' she said firmly, probably realising that announcing her married name to his parents' employees might not be the most diplomatic of moves.

'Welcome to Villa des Lufttals, Ruby.'

'Thank you. The villa is *amazing*!'

George's chest puffed out. He looked as delighted by her praise as if he were personally responsible for it all. Mind you, George and his wife, Ursula, had been with them for twenty-four years, and kept the château running like a well-oiled machine.

'I trust Veronika and Mathias are both well,' he said, asking after George and Ursula's children.

'Very well. They send their love.'

'And give them mine.'

George took their coats. 'Now, your parents are waiting for you in the blue drawing room.'

Luis stumbled. 'My parents are here?'

'But of course. They are eager to see you and meet Miss… Ruby.' George raised a meaningful eyebrow. 'You have never brought a woman home before. You have them...'

'Agog?' he muttered.

'Worried,' Ruby murmured for his ears only.

'Delighted,' George countered.

A heavy weight settled on his shoulders. What had changed? Why could his parents no longer let him be to live his life the way he saw fit? Rubbing a hand across his chest, he tried to ease the tightness there. What was truly behind his mother's desire to see him married?

Straightening, he glanced at Ruby. She would help him put an end to all of this folly, he would find out what was at the heart of his mother's demands, he would somehow address them, and then things could go back to how they had been.

Ruby's eyes widened as they followed George through the series of rooms and corridors that led from the villa's back entrance and towards the blue drawing room, her gaze darting everywhere. Glancing up, she caught his gaze and slapped his arm—not hard, but not quite playfully either. 'I thought we came through the back door,' she whispered.

'We did.'

'Then what's all this *splendour*?'

He halted to stare about the room they currently passed through. She thought it splendid? He supposed it was. 'This is a small breakfast room that is often used in the summer as it has access to that pretty little courtyard there.' He glanced back behind him. 'That was a games room, but is rarely used these days unless we're having a house party. There is also a small music room and sitting room along here before we come to the larger reception rooms.'

'Luis, there's nothing *small* about any of this.'

He tried to see it through her eyes but it was too familiar. He knew every nook and cranny, every stair that creaked and every window that rattled when the wind came from the north. He knew which rooms provided the coolest spots in the summer and the cosiest spots in the winter. He didn't notice the grandness. It was just *home*.

But did all of this come with a price tag he hadn't realised he'd have to pay—like marriage?

Swallowing, he dragged himself back into the moment. 'I suppose splendour is dependent on scale.'

'So the blue drawing room?'

'Very grand. We rarely use it in winter unless we're entertaining.' The blue drawing room *and* they'd taken the day off work—his parents must want to impress Ruby. Things inside him drew tight, but he stiffened his spine. It was time all of this marriage nonsense was put to bed.

Ushering her out of the room, he gave a grand flourish. 'This is the entrance hall. It's what you would've first seen if we'd entered through the front door.' A thing he rarely did.

She turned on the spot, mouth hanging open. Tilting her head back, she stared at the vaulted ceiling, the heavily carved wooden panelling that lined the walls, the cast-iron grillwork that framed the staircase. She stared at Luis, raising both hands, before turning to George, who nodded. 'I agree, madam.'

'Ruby,' she corrected absently.

'It is a pleasure to work here.'

Luis frowned. Had he started to take all of this for granted? He knew he was fortunate, but—

'Luis, is that you?'

Claudia Keller's upright figure appeared in a doorway to the right. Dragging in a breath, he tucked Ruby's hand into the crook of his elbow. Her fingers dug into the fine wool of his jumper and held on as if life itself depended on it. He patted it, trying to let her know she wasn't alone. To his relief, she kept a game smile on her lips and her chin high as he led her across to his mother.

He kissed his mother's cheek. Easing back, he gestured to the woman at his side. 'Mutti, I'd like you to meet, Ruby.'

'It's lovely to meet you, Mrs Keller.' Before his mother could reply, Ruby clasped her hands beneath her chin. 'I have never seen a more beautiful home,' she gushed. 'Luis said he came from a well-to-do family, but you guys must be *really* rich.'

Behind them, George coughed. Only someone who knew his mother well would've clocked her surprise and noticed the way her eyes fractionally widened. 'I'm glad you like it, my dear.'

Ruby sent them both a 'cat who got the cream' kind of smile and all Luis could do was stare. Gone was the warm and lovely woman he'd met in Vegas, replaced instead with a bumbling and perhaps conniving woman—the scales teetering between ingenue and calculation.

'Thank you so much for having me here, Mrs Keller. I can't wait to see the rest of your beautiful house and see all of the beautiful things you own and—'

'Any friend of Luis's is always welcome at Villa des Lufttals,' his mother smoothly broke in as if to cut off any further gushing. 'And please, Ruby, you must call me Claudia. Come and meet Walter.'

Claudia took her arm, but they didn't make it five steps inside the drawing room before Ruby dragged them to a halt. 'Is that a *real* suit of armour?'

'Yes, we call him Gerhardt.'

'It must be priceless!'

His mother frowned. 'It is a museum piece, certainly.'

They made it a further two steps before Ruby halted again. 'Oh, my God, is that a Monet?'

'A Pissarro,' Claudia murmured.

Luis wasn't entirely sure all of Ruby's awe was feigned.

'And those vases?' She pointed.

'Are pretty, don't you think, dear?'

Ruby nodded, her dark hair bouncing. 'But I expect they're antiques. I'm not going anywhere near them in case I should bump them.'

The alarm in her voice had him moving up beside her. 'Ruby, these are just things.'

'Uh-huh, but if I break any of the things in my or my parents' houses, I can pop down to the discount department store and replace them. I'm thinking that's not going to be the case here.' She sent his mother a weak smile. 'I certainly won't be wearing my roller skates inside your house.'

'You...roller skate?' his mother said faintly.

'Oh, yes, it's my favourite thing in the world!'

Luis couldn't utter a single word for fear of laughing. If he'd had any doubts about Ruby's ability to pull this off, she'd just put them all to rest. She was truly awful—gauche, with not just dollar signs in her eyes, but stars as well. She walked an inspired line between awestruck and money-hungry. He had to pin his arms to his sides so as not to applaud her.

His mother urged her forward again. 'Walter, this is Ruby. Luis's...friend.'

'Welcome, Ruby. Do not let the house frighten you.' He patted her hand. 'We've all had an accident or two over the years.'

Luis held his breath. His father's warmth could undo most people, but Ruby kept up her façade. Beaming at him and Claudia, she said, 'I think it's amazing that the two of you have remained such good friends after having been married. If I ever divorce, I hope it will be as amicable as yours.'

Except, perhaps, that was a step too far. Luis broke the sudden and fraught silence with a quick, 'Amen!'

Wrapping an arm around Ruby's shoulders, he planted a huge grin to his face and hoped he looked truly and utterly smitten. 'Mutti and Vati…' Unexpected nerves gathered in his chest. 'We were going to announce it at dinner tonight as I didn't expect to see you before then, but…'

His throat went dry.

'Luis?' his mother prompted when he didn't continue.

He cleared his throat. 'While we were in Vegas…'

Both of his parents leaned towards him, not an ounce of suspicion flickering in their eyes. *Verdammt*, maybe this wasn't such a good idea.

Ruby slipped an arm around his waist and squeezed, and he straightened. He needed to get to the bottom of whatever it was that was driving his mother's marriage ambition for him, and put an end to it. 'Well, the thing was, as soon as I laid eyes on Ruby, I knew she was the one.'

The smiles on Claudia's and Walter's faces froze.

He grinned down at Ruby—made it a truly goofy grin. 'And as we were in Vegas…'

It hadn't occurred to him that he'd find it so

hard to lie to his parents. Though, technically, it wasn't a lie. He and Ruby *were* married.

Ruby leapt in. 'What Luis is trying to say is that when in Vegas…do as those who go to Vegas do.'

Claudia planted her hands on her hips. 'What are the two of you talking about?'

Ruby held up her left hand to display her wedding ring at the same time as he said, 'Ruby and I got married.'

They gaped at him.

The collar of his shirt tightened, but he ignored it. 'As I said, I knew the moment I clapped eyes on Ruby that she was the one. There didn't seem any point in waiting. We figured it was…'

'Fate,' Ruby finished for him. She bounced on the spot. 'Isn't it the most beautiful ring you've ever seen?'

The silence that sounded in the room had Ruby's arm tightening about him. Wisely, though, she didn't utter another word. He hitched up his chin. 'Mutti and Vati, aren't you going to congratulate us?'

Claudia immediately shook herself. 'Of course!' Reaching across, she pulled Ruby into a hug. When she released her, Ruby swayed as if a little drunk. She glanced at him, something stricken in her eyes. But then his father was shaking his hand, and his mother was hugging him too, and they were ushing them to the sofas by the fire and demanding to hear their tale, and there was no chance to ask her if she was okay.

'There's not much more to tell,' he said. 'We spent the week together when Ruby wasn't busy with her conference and just…clicked. When the week came to an end—' he sent her another goofy smile '—we couldn't bear to part.'

'It was *so* romantic,' Ruby gushed. 'Luis took me out dancing and we played blackjack and drank *really expensive* champagne and just… perhaps we did drink a little too much bubbly— and the tequila shots were definitely a mistake. But on the spur of the moment we decided to have one of those fake wedding services—a bit of silliness to get the full Vegas experience.'

Walter rubbed a hand over his face. Claudia simply stared as if she had no idea what to say. 'The full Vegas experience?' she finally said.

'Oh, yes!' Ruby nodded. 'The whole fake wedding gown and a dime-store ring, and with an Elvis impersonator officiating.'

He choked back a laugh. Ruby was right. They needed to make this sound as terrible as they could. The shock alone had to send fault lines fracturing through his mother's emotional armour. Once it was cracked, he'd be able to keep chipping away until it all fell away and he discovered the truth.

Hopefully Claudia would then be so relieved when he dissolved the marriage, she'd never hassle him to marry again. 'It was a hoot, but afterwards we couldn't help thinking we ought to do the real deal.'

'Luis bought me this gorgeous ring—with not just one, but *three diamonds*—went down on one knee and promised me a white Christmas in his castle in the Swiss Alps if I'd marry him. I mean, it was so fairy-tale perfect how was a girl to resist?'

'And that's how we woke up married in Vegas,' Luis finished.

He didn't blame his parents for their stunned silence.

His mother gazed down at her hands. 'I can't pretend I'm not disappointed to have not been at your wedding, Luis.'

His lips twisted. 'In all the time you've been badgering me to get married, Mutti, not once did you mention that you also wanted a grand wedding.'

'It didn't have to be grand.' Her stricken expression pierced him to the marrow. 'It's just... I always expected to be there.' She lifted her chin, but her smile didn't reach her eyes. 'What I *can* say from the bottom of my heart, though, is that I wish you both every happiness.' She swung to Walter. 'You'll need to bring up a bottle of our finest champagne from the cellar so we can toast the happy couple at dinner. I'm going to talk to Ursula and have the yellow suite readied for Luis and his bride.'

Luis shot to his feet. 'There's nothing wrong with my current room.'

'My dear Luis, you're a married man. You and your new wife will need more room. This is in effect your honeymoon, and I mean to rise to the occasion.'

CHAPTER THREE

LUIS HELD HIS finger to his lips as the door closed behind them. Ruby twisted her hands together, her stomach performing one sick somersault after another. With an apologetic grimace, he began kissing the back of his hand and made lip-smacking sounds, and her eyes bugged. What—? *Oh!*

Wincing, she uttered a breathy moan, and an 'Oh, Luis…', her body shimmying as if—

Oh, God, don't finish that thought!

She just needed to make it sound as if she were truly kissing Luis. If someone had their ear pressed to the door, as Luis clearly feared, they needed to convince them they were embarking on married life with every evidence of passion.

Taking her arm, he led her from the cosy sitting room, through a doorway, and into an enormous bedroom. With a four-poster bed draped in the lushest yellow brocade. Staring at that bed had her chest clenching. Shooting across the room to the window, she hoped Luis simply thought her eager to see the view when what she needed to do was put as much distance between them as she could.

The window looked out over an orchard, the branches of the trees winter bare, snow all around. Beyond, large mountains rose. All of it was breathtaking.

'This is a corner suite, and this room doesn't share a wall with the corridor outside.'

Meaning it would be almost impossible for anyone to hear them in here. Turning back, she nodded. 'Right.'

Two doors on the far wall gave her something to do. Opening the first, she found an enormous dressing room. The second was the en suite bathroom, but she'd never seen an en suite of such grand dimensions.

She was aware of Luis's gaze on her, heavy and watchful…expectant. It took all her strength to turn towards him. 'I'm sorry,' she said.

At the same time as he said, 'I apologise most sincerely.'

They both blinked.

'What are you apologising for?' they asked at the same time.

Clicking his tongue, Luis took her hand and led her to the padded bench that ran along the base of the bed. 'Tell me what you are apologising for.'

She buried her face in her hands. 'God, I was awful! Your poor parents.'

'You were perfection,' he countered.

When she lifted her head, one glorious eyebrow lifted. 'Roller skating?'

She gave a silent scream. 'I have no idea what came over me. I haven't roller skated since I was a kid. It just popped into my head and—' She mimed vomiting. 'Your parents must be appalled.'

'But this is the plan, yes? That is what I mean. You were perfection.'

She gnawed on her bottom lip. 'I guess. I just… Your parents are lovely. I thought they'd be awful.'

He blinked. 'What did I say to give you that impression?'

'I thought that, given the way your mother was pressuring you, they'd be…'

'Harsh and uncaring? Cold?'

She wrinkled her nose, ashamed at her own short-sightedness.

'Which would make lying to them easier.'

The despondent slope of his shoulders had her crashing back. She ought to be making things as easy as she could for him. He'd promised that she'd win her partnership. She was in Switzerland, *in a castle*, for heaven's sake. She was having a long-overdue adventure. She had nothing to bellyache about.

'I'm glad they're not. I'm glad they're lovely. I wish my own parents—' She cut that thought dead. 'Don't worry, I'm not having second thoughts. It's just…odd to act so awful without apologising for it.' Recalling how he'd gone out of his way to cheer her up in Vegas, she made herself grin. 'So if all goes to plan this probably won't be the first time I apologise when we're alone. Now tell me why—'

'What happened between you and my mother?'

She blinked. 'When?'

'When she was congratulating us, and she hugged you. Did she say something?'

To her horror her eyes filled.

He seized both of her hands. 'You must tell me. My mother isn't usually cruel but if she said something to upset you—'

'It was nothing like that. Besides, after that performance neither of us could blame her if she forgot her manners for a moment.'

The way his lips firmed told her he didn't agree. 'If it wasn't that…?'

She swallowed the lump that wanted to lodge in her throat. 'She hugged me like she meant it. Even though I was awful and have to be the last thing she'd want for her son, she still hugged me with all of herself.'

She couldn't remember the last time her mother had hugged her like that. 'I wasn't expecting it. It took me off guard.' It had made her feel like an absolute heel.

'She hugged me like that too.'

Yeah, but he'd been expecting it.

Warm lips lifted. 'I'm glad she made you feel welcome.'

Oh, this was so messed up! She leaped to her feet and paced back to the window. Luis loved his parents and they clearly adored him. Why was a deception of this magnitude necessary? Why was his mother pushing him so hard to marry when she had to know it was the last thing he wanted?

Turning back, she rested against the window frame. 'Tell me why you apologised just now?'

He swept an arm around the room. 'For this. It didn't occur to me that we would be expected to share a bedroom. I hadn't considered the *logistics*. And now—'

'I did.'

He blinked.

'We're newly-weds, Luis. Of course your family expects us to share a room and a bed. But we agreed back in Vegas that was only going to be for show.' A pulse ticced in her throat. 'Is that going to be a problem for you?'

He dragged a hand through his hair. 'Of course not.'

But neither of them could look the other in the eye.

'So…' His swallow was audible. 'How did you think we'd *negotiate* sharing a room?'

'We've been given a whole suite! We've oodles of room.' Walking back into the sitting room, she pointed at the sofa. 'I'll sleep there.'

He stiffened. 'You'll do nothing of the sort. *I'll* sleep there.'

'But your feet will hang over the end whereas I'll—'

'*I* will take the sofa,' he repeated.

Rolling her eyes, she threw up a hand. 'Fine, whatever. If you change your mind, just say the word.' She eyed him for a moment. 'We could take it turn about.'

'No.'

Hovering in the doorway to the bedroom again, she took in the size of the bed—huge. If they placed a bolster of pillows down the middle of it…

Swinging away she shook her head.

'No,' he agreed, his eyes dark, as if he'd read what she'd been thinking. 'I'll take the sofa.'

'Okey-doke,' she squeaked, relieved when her phone pinged. 'That's the notification for my work email.'

'Excellent.' Luis lowered himself to the sofa. 'What do they say?'

She moved to sit beside him. Not too close, though, as she still couldn't shake the vision of that four-poster bed next door from her mind. 'Da de dah…' She scrolled down. 'They say they understand my disappointment at their recent decision to not make me a partner.'

They both snorted.

'But that I'm a valued member of the team—' her brows rose '—and to reflect that, they're offering me a pay rise.'

Luis folded his arms. 'And what *aren't* you going to do?'

'I'm not going to answer any of my work emails for the next week,' she recited.

'Exactly. Besides, as soon as they see the announcement in the paper tomorrow—'

'What announcement?'

'Our marriage announcement. It will make the national news in both the society pages and financial pages—and will garner some international attention as well.'

Her mouth opened and closed, but not a single word emerged.

'I'm not a renowned playboy, by any means. I rarely attend A-list parties, and I keep my dates low-key. But as I'm considered one of Europe's most eligible bachelors, my marriage will be considered news.' He stared at her. 'I mean to deliver on what I promised, Ruby. You will have the offer of a partnership before you leave Switzerland.'

It had all seemed so simple when they'd concocted this plan in Vegas two days ago, but now...

But now nothing! She wanted that partnership. She'd *earned* it. She would prove to everyone that she *wasn't* a failure.

'I'd better inform my parents of my unexpected marriage sooner rather than later, then.'

He rose. 'I'll give you some privacy.'

'No, no. Before you go, we need to come up with a better plan. Me being a gold-digging harpy isn't going to be enough. Your mother is too big-hearted for that.'

He gaped at her. 'Are you kidding me? You're her worst nightmare.'

Oh, how she wished that were true. She recalled again the way Claudia had hugged her and had to swallow. 'They love you, which means they'll accept someone like me for your sake. Even if they don't like it.'

He sat again, rubbed a hand over his face.

Dragging in a breath, she let it out slowly. She *could* do this. 'I not only need to be their worst nightmare,' she started slowly, 'but we need them to think I'm yours too. If they think I'm ruining your life, *that's* what will spur them to action.' And that was what would help him get to the heart of this mystery. 'We need them to think I'm *bad* for you.'

Behind the glorious blue of his eyes, she sensed his mind racing. 'That's a clever strategy. You could be onto something.'

Even though she tried to stop it, her chest puffed out a bit.

Stop being pathetic.

'What does your mother want from your marriage?'

'What do you mean?'

'She must *want* something if she's been pushing you so hard. Like… I don't know, did she want you to marry money?'

That had him shaking his head. 'We've enough of our own.'

'Status?'

'Again, unlikely.'

'Okay, what about children?'

He shrugged. 'I don't know. I suppose she might like some of those.'

'Fine, from here on children are anathema to me.'

'Do you dislike children?'

'Of course not. They're lovely. But that's neither here nor there. For the next month, I consider them horrid and completely unnecessary.'

His lips twitched. 'What is my reaction to this supposed to be?'

'Oh, you're going to give me everything I want because you're completely under my spell. You've no spine where I'm concerned.'

The twitching became a full-blown grin. 'They'd hate to see me like that.'

'But whenever children are mentioned, try and look a little forlorn.'

'Forbearing but wistful?'

'Exactly! Think you're up for it?'

'Absolutely.'

She considered the problem some more. 'How important is work to your family?'

'It is our bedrock. We all work for Keller Enterprises—the family company. My father is CEO, my mother is Human Resources Manager, while I'm in charge of the new technology arm we're developing.'

She raised her eyebrows.

'No! I couldn't leave the company. I'd—'

'I'm not saying you have to leave, but if for the next month your parents think there's a possibility that you might relocate to Australia for an unforeseen length of time, maybe to back me in some project that's dear to my heart...' She'd make sure that project sounded like a total disaster too—something that would appal them.

Leaning his elbows on his knees, he rested his face in his hands. 'It would hurt them, worry them. They'd hate it.'

It was clear he'd hate it too. She touched his shoulder. 'We don't have to do that. I'm just throwing ideas out there.'

He lifted his head, determination settling across his features. 'No, you're right, this is the perfect plan. I need to change into someone they barely recognise. Something is wrong.' His hands clenched. 'I can grit my teeth for the next month to find out what that is.'

He hadn't expected it to be this hard, she could see that now. Ruthless wasn't Luis's default setting. He liked to take care of people, not distress them.

Blue eyes arrowed to hers. 'Right, we're anti-children, there's the possibility of me leaving the family business to pursue other interests...

Is there anything else you can think of that would appropriately horrify them?'

Her stomach gave a sick lurch. 'I never knew I could be so devious, but yes. What about friends?'

'You want to appal my friends too?'

'No, I want your parents to think I'm smothering you, that I'm being controlling. Is there a regular thing you do? You know, like a poker night or—'

'Hockey. I play ice hockey. It's just a social comp, but whenever I'm not travelling, I play.' He met her gaze, grimaced. 'But not for the next month.'

She sent him a weak smile. 'Which is a shame. I'd have loved to see you play.'

He blinked. 'You would?'

Dear God, did she have some stupid dreamy expression on her face? She did her best to not look like an infatuated teenager. 'I've never been to an ice-hockey game.'

Luis stared into Ruby's lovely hazel eyes, and immediately starting plotting how he could take her to a hockey game.

'I can see what you're thinking, but forget it,' she ordered. 'We're here to get a job done, not give me the full tourist experience.'

He would like her to have fun while she was here, though. They could achieve what they wanted *and* have fun. There was no law against it. He pushed his shoulders back. Before she left Switzerland, he would surprise her with an ice-hockey game. Somehow.

The thought of Ruby leaving, though, had the weight slamming back to his shoulders. He didn't want to be married—he had zero intention of remaining married—but having Ruby here made him feel less alone. It was nice to have her in his corner. 'You know that thing you said about me backing you in some project dear to your heart?'

'Hmm…?'

'Is that such a bad idea?'

Her head snapped back. 'It's a terrible idea.'

'Why?'

'Because you're already doing so much for me.'

That had him gaping. 'So much…?'

'Yes! You're helping me get the partnership—not to mention mentoring me in negotiation skills while we're at it—*and* you're giving me this amazing holiday in Switzerland.'

A holiday where she wouldn't let him take her to a hockey match.

She rolled her eyes mock dramatically. 'You've saved me from a Christmas of Christa's gloating and my family's not so silent disappointment. Instead I'm getting the full white-Christmas experience, and in a castle no less.'

It prickled him that her parents couldn't see what a talented daughter they had. How could they not appreciate her?

Last week in Vegas he'd have made some amusing comment that would've had her laughing. This week he let the silence hang until she shifted on the sofa and glanced away.

'I didn't mean backing you in some project dear to your heart *and* helping you score the partnership. I meant instead of.'

She swung back, her eyes bugging.

'What if you were to strike out on your own? What if you were to start your own law firm?'

'On my own? Are you *mad*?'

Over the years, her family had whittled away her confidence, and the senior executives at her firm had done nothing to improve it. He couldn't explain why, but he wanted to build her up and make her see herself as he saw her. 'Why not? I'd be happy to back you. You've the drive, the experience and the intelligence to make a success of any such venture.'

She laughed—a weird, high-pitched, completely disbelieving sound. 'You're vastly overestimating my skill set.'

He leapt up and stormed from one side of the room to the other. 'Rather than taking a risk, you'd prefer to work for a firm that doesn't value your hard work or the sacrifices you make?'

He picked up a brass bust—a likeness of someone he supposed he ought to know—and glared at it, before dropping it back to the mantelpiece. 'You would rather remain there and be taken advantage of than seeing how high you could actually climb?' He slammed his hands to his hips. 'No wonder they didn't give you that partnership! Why should they value you when you don't value yourself?'

She'd risen too, probably in an effort to stop from feeling so small, and she now held folded arms against her chest like a shield, watching him silently with big, wounded eyes. Remorse pierced him. She was alone in a foreign country, she'd known him little more than a week, and here he was ranting at her like some bully.

Bracing hands on his knees, he dragged in a breath. 'I'm sorry, Ruby.' Straightening, he strode across and pulled her into a hug. 'I'm sorry. I had no right to speak like that. And, anyway, I lied. I would've given you the promotion. I saw how hard you worked. You deserved it.'

Wrapping his arms around her shoulders, he held her gently against his chest, ready to release her the moment she indicated that his touch was unwelcome. After a moment, she relaxed against him, her arms going around his waist, and she hugged him back. It felt like a gift.

And then he had to grit his teeth against the rush of heat that flooded his veins as her softness and her scent wrapped around him. 'Say you forgive me?'

'Of course I forgive you,' she mumbled against

his shoulder. 'Emotions are running high. It's only natural for things to get tense.'

'Perhaps, but I promised to be a friend to you.' His arms tightened. 'Also, I dislike your firm immensely. The thought of you going back to work for a group that don't value you the way you ought to be valued is abhorrent to me. But I've no right to make any such judgement. That decision is not mine to make.'

She gave him a soft squeeze and then eased away, not meeting his eyes as she tucked her hair behind her ears. He immediately missed her warmth, and the way he felt anchored when she was in his arms. 'You see me too kindly.'

'While you do not see yourself kindly enough.' At her swift glance, though, he raised his hands. 'However, as they say in America, we will park this conversation for another day.'

She smiled, but it didn't reach her eyes. 'There really isn't anything to talk about, Luis. I've no intention of striking out on my own. Do you know how many new businesses fail within the first three years? The thought of failing so spectacularly and proving my family right…' She shuddered.

She had been surrounded by people who hadn't appreciated her for far too long. It was time that changed. Maybe they ought to extend this arrangement of theirs for another month so he could return to Australia with her and force them all to see her in a new light. He'd ponder that when he had the time. Glancing at his watch now, though, he said, 'There's three hours till dinner with my parents.'

She pointed a finger at him. 'The *celebratory* dinner with your parents, thank you very much.'

They'd have to be in their finest form. 'You must be tired after the travelling, plus you need to ring your family. Why don't you do that, and then try to get some rest?'

Warm eyes raked his face, luscious lips pursed and then she smiled and it felt as if someone had hit him with a hockey stick in the chest. 'Remember what I said before we left Vegas—this coming month *can* be fun. It doesn't all have to be fraught and stressful.'

They'd certainly had a lot of fun in Vegas. And then he recalled the kind of fun that had landed them here and a bolt of heat threaded through his bloodstream, pooling in parts of his anatomy he needed to keep on ice.

'I know we're going to shock your parents and that it'll be uncomfortable for them—and probably for us too—but they haven't exactly made things comfortable for you recently either. We're not motivated by either spite or greed, so I think it's okay to dispense with the guilt.'

She had a point. It was just… Ever since his parents' divorce when he was fourteen years old, he'd done his best to look after them.

His stomach churned at the memory. It had been an awful time, the worst time of his life. He'd been consumed with worry, sitting outside his mother's bedroom door listening to her weep, his heart burning, appalled at how pale and thin she'd grown. His father too had lost weight, growing gaunt and grey. When months had passed and nothing had changed he'd grown even more fearful, at a loss for how to ease their pain and help them find their feet again.

Eventually he'd resorted to cajoling and bullying his mother into the kitchen, telling her that Walter missed her *kuchen* and begging her to teach him how to make it. That had galvanised her into action. He'd then cajoled Walter into eating it by telling him that Claudia had made it for him especially. Walter had cleaned up every crumb.

He'd dragged his father out into the garden to help him build a rose garden, telling him Claudia had said she'd wanted one. A strategy that had won his father's complete cooperation and full focus. When he told Claudia about it, she'd practically raced outside to admire the result.

Slowly his parents had started eating again, had started getting out in the sun and exercising, took pains to thank and compliment each other. They'd slowly cemented the friendship they now enjoyed, and Luis had been able to breathe freely once more. But he'd sworn to himself in those long dark months to never put himself through such turmoil. It had all been utterly exhausting. Why would anyone willingly put themselves through that?

Now he could see that he'd fallen into the habit of not creating waves or causing drama. Of not hurting or disappointing them. Unlike Ruby and her family, though, he knew his parents had appreciated his efforts. But where had it got him?

With his mother now demanding he marry, and his father on the sidelines pleading neutrality. It wasn't reasonable. And it wasn't kind. But had he been the one to teach them to treat him like that? 'I think, Ruby, I was a very odd teenager—*weird.*'

Walking across, Ruby took his hand, squeezed it. 'I don't think you're weird. I think you're lovely.'

Their gazes locked and held, heat arced between them, but before it could turn into a full-blown fire, she tore her gaze from his and stepped away. Striding across to the mantelpiece, she picked up that brass bust. 'Why do you say you were odd?'

The air between them throbbed. He did his best to ignore it. 'I never rebelled.' Weren't all teenagers supposed to rebel?

'I don't think I did either.'

He'd bet Christa was at the bottom of that. 'What did you do instead?'

'I tried to make myself invisible.' Slim shoulders lifted. 'It's a weird time, being a teenager, isn't it?

I just wanted peace and quiet. And I mostly got it, so my strategy worked. Why didn't you rebel?'

He hesitated. 'I was fourteen when my parents divorced. They were both so hurt, but putting on such brave faces for each other.' His heart had bled for them. 'I didn't want them putting on a brave face for me too.' He hadn't had the heart to put them through that on top of everything else. 'It was important to them to remain friends—and important to me too—and I guess I didn't want to do anything that would ruin that.'

She made as if to move towards him—as if she wanted to hug him—but pulled to a sudden and awkward halt. All of the spaces between them throbbed with an underlying awareness, and from the way she momentarily glanced away, he knew she felt it too.

'Luis, I think you're the kindest person I've ever met.'

Her words made him blink.

She lifted that pointed chin. 'Maybe it's time we both rebelled.'

'Aren't we a little old for that?'

'Absolutely not! You have every right to rebel against a dictate to marry.'

Her words had things inside him firing to life. If he had taught his parents to treat him as if he would always submit to their demands, then it was time to teach them otherwise. They were all adults, and they certainly didn't need him acting as a go-between any more.

He met her gaze. 'And what will you be rebelling against?'

She folded her arms. 'My parents believe me a screw-up—someone who's never lived up to her potential—so maybe it's time I gave them a reason to think that.' Her mouth kinked upwards. 'Maybe I'll start living in the moment and stop trying to win their approval.'

Excellent plan!

She rubbed her hands together. 'This is how the rest of my day is going to go. I'm going to ring my parents and absolutely appal them with the story of my reckless and oh-so-hasty marriage, then blithely tell them I won't be home for Christmas. Which will be a total shock as, somehow, I end up doing most of the work on the day.'

Why did that not surprise him?

'After a rejuvenating rest and a long soak in that glorious bathtub…'

She pointed in the direction of their bathroom and he did everything he could not to imagine her stretched out naked in the bath with steam rising all around her and the water beading on her flawless skin.

Verdammt! He hauled his mind back to find her tapping a finger against her chin.

'And tonight I'll put on the show of my life and be the kind of woman your parents will never be able to love, no matter how hard they try.' She winked at him. 'While you will simply be too smitten to see what a horror I am. We'll be a train wreck they can't look away from. They're going to realise how wonderful everything was before you were married, and wonder what kind of mess they've pressured you into. When this is over, you'll get your peace back and everyone will be happy again. It doesn't sound like such a bad plan, does it?'

It didn't sound like a bad plan at all. He rubbed his hands together too. 'Game on.'

CHAPTER FOUR

LUIS COLLAPSED ONTO the sofa in the sitting room of their suite and stared into the fire that crackled softly in the fireplace. He barely had the energy to breathe. That dinner had been *exhausting*.

Ruby fell down beside him. 'Oh, God, that was awful. *I* was awful!'

Reaching across, he squeezed her hand. 'You were superb.' Wonderfully and awfully superb. Not malicious or spiteful or mean. Just gloriously and ruthlessly self-centred.

'Did you see the expression on your mother's face when I oh-so-blithely told her you wouldn't be returning to work until some time in January?'

He winced.

'She looked as if I'd slapped her. It was all I could do not to backtrack and tell her I'd have you in the office first thing tomorrow.'

Resting his head against the sofa, he said, 'You should win an acting award. You looked totally unmoved.'

Her eyes widened. 'Really?'

Her surprise made him smile. 'Really.'

They were silent for a little while, staring into the flames and letting the crackling of the fire soothe shattered nerves. Eventually, though, he felt the weight of Ruby's stare. He turned his head, raised an eyebrow.

She bit the inside of her cheek. 'Your mother is going to be a hard nut to crack. Why didn't she put me in my place, tell me to back off or tell me to shut up and let you answer for yourself?'

'That's not really her style.'

'She's the head of Keller Enterprises' HR division, Luis. She'd know how to shut someone down.'

'But that's work and this…isn't. She's probably still reeling from the news we're married.'

'I guess.'

He shifted. 'Would you have preferred it if I'd been more active?' He'd done nothing except sit there with a stupidly besotted expression on his face. He'd felt like an idiot. It was Ruby who'd done all the heavy lifting.

'No! You were brilliant! Didn't you see their expressions whenever you patted my hand and said, *"Whatever you want, Ruby"* in answer to all the nonsense I was spouting? They were gobsmacked.'

He grinned. 'Like when you said you thought our en suite would benefit from the addition of gold taps. What on earth put that into your head?'

'One of the hotels in Vegas had them. I overhead someone at the conference talking about them. I thought they'd be the kind of thing Bad Ruby would love.'

They were silent again for a while.

'When your father asked where we were planning to live, you fobbed him off.'

He'd just… 'I thought we'd given them enough surprises for one day. I thought it'd be more effective if we spaced the shocks out.'

'A bit like Chinese water torture?' She rubbed her hands together—not so much in relish but as if to try and warm them up. 'We'll drip-drip away until they beg for mercy. Your mother is going to be *so* happy when you break up with me.'

He rubbed a hand over his face. It didn't sit well with him that his parents would come to loathe Ruby. Not when the real Ruby was so warm and funny and generous. He couldn't have it both ways, though. If they *did* know her, it'd ruin everything.

'Your parents must love you a lot if they're prepared to put up with me with such good grace.'

He closed his eyes and counted to three. 'I know they love me, Ruby.'

'But?'

He opened his eyes again and met hers squarely. 'Family is a place where one should be loved and accepted for who they are.'

Her lips twisted. 'It should be.'

'A place where the people should support each other.'

'Uh-huh.'

'Supported is the last thing I feel. Until recently, I thought I had a good relationship with my parents. I thought they had my best interests at heart.' In the same way he'd always had their best interests at heart. 'Something changed when I wasn't paying attention. They've become ruthless in the same way your alter ego is ruthless. They want what they want regardless of the expense to me.' It rocked him to his very foundations.

'There has to be a reason.'

'But what?'

She thrust out her chin. 'We're smart. Given time, we'll work it out.'

He started to laugh. This woman—she was amazing. In lots of ways. Continually surprising him and—

Unbidden, that four-poster bed in the room next door rose in his mind making things surge and swell inside him. Hell. He needed to put some distance between him and it.

'Are you tired?'

Her brows rose at whatever she saw in his face. 'No, why?'

'I'm in the mood for dancing.' He wanted to wear himself out until he was certain he'd sleep and be too tired to consider…anything else.

Her eyes lit up. 'Really?'

'And in the morning, we can sleep as late as we want, which is *very* out of character for me.'

'Sold!'

They made a lot noise as they drunkenly let themselves into the villa, via the front door this time because Luis had insisted she get the full effect of that grand foyer, and because he'd *wanted* to make noise. A *lot* of noise. Apparently this would demonstrate a lack of respect for anyone else in the house, further illustrating Ruby's bad influence on him.

Ruby wasn't drunk, but she might be a tiny bit tipsy, and as the full grandeur of the villa once again slammed into her, her disbelief had her giggles practically becoming belly laughs. Oh, that staircase…the vaulted ceiling…the—

Oops. Both of Luis's parents stood on the first-floor landing. She tapped his arm and pointed. Even from this distance, she could see the way Claudia's eyes narrowed.

'Do you know what time it is, Luis?' Walter demanded.

Yes, they did, thank you very much. Mission accomplished! It wouldn't hurt to drive that particular nail home again and again, though. Clutching Luis's arm, Ruby peered up into his face, swaying slightly. 'Switzerland is known for its clocks and watches, isn't it? It's like the timepiece capital of the world.' She curled into his side, hopefully seductively, and waved her left wrist under his nose. 'Sweetie pie, I don't have a watch. Will you buy me a Rolex? I've always wanted one.'

His arm went around her. 'First thing tomorrow, *meine kleine Zaubermaus*.'

She choked back a laugh at what sounded like a truly ridiculous endearment. 'Your parents look outraged,' she stage-whispered. 'Haven't you ever stumbled home in the wee small hours before?'

She *really* needed to make Claudia and Walter loathe her.

She ground her teeth together. What she *wasn't* going to do was drop to her knees and beg them to forgive her appalling behaviour.

'I usually stay at my apartment in Zurich when I have a night on the town. Especially if I'm with a girl.'

Not that they'd had a 'night on the town'. Not really. She'd had a couple of drinks and they'd danced their excess energy away at a ski lodge further up the mountain. Being wrapped so close to him now, though, reminded her why they'd both had so much excess energy to begin with.

The dancing, while a distraction, had done nothing to ease her body's burn for Luis. The blood in her veins ran with a constant heat, as if she had a fever. She couldn't very well unwrap herself from around him now, though, not without ruining the impression she was trying to make.

She made herself giggle. 'But I'm not just any

girl.' She made her eyes comically wide. 'I'm your wife.'

Luis's eyes filled with mirth and he started to laugh as if he couldn't help it. And then she started laughing. And then neither of them could stop. They had to hold onto each other to remain upright. The release in tension was glorious, so she had no idea why she wanted to cry.

'Luis,' his mother said in a long-suffering tone. 'Please tell me you didn't drive home.'

'I was fine to drive,' he said. 'Ruby was cold. Couldn't keep her waiting.'

In the sudden silence, he belched, and rubbed his stomach. 'I'm not sure that bratwurst agreed with me.'

Ruby rubbed his back. 'Are you going to be sick, babe?'

When she glanced back up, both of his parents had gone.

'That went ridiculously well,' he whispered for her ears only.

It had. She didn't know whether to feel *really* bad about it. Or not.

But then Luis picked her up and swung her around. 'You are amazing! Perfect! Magic!'

Nobody had ever thought those things about her before. Just for a moment she let herself savour the warmth and strength in the oh-so-masculine body beneath her fingertips, before he set her back on her feet.

Heart beating furiously and pulse racing like a mad thing, she tucked her hair behind her ears and tried to look unflustered. *"'Meine kleine Zaubermaus?'"*

'My little magic mouse.'

She clapped a hand over her mouth to contain a snort of laughter. 'Best endearment ever!'

They chuckled all the way up the stairs. When they reached their rooms, she hurried to grab him a blanket from the bed. He stood in the doorway, waiting, but didn't step across the threshold. She passed the blanket to him, her mouth going dry.

'Sweet Ruby.' His hand lifted as if to touch her cheek, but he lowered it again. He nodded at the door. 'Close that.'

'What if you need the bathroom?'

But he'd already turned away. 'Close the door, Ruby.'

She closed the door.

Luis was nowhere to be seen when Ruby woke the next morning. Showered and dressed, she hesitated. What was she supposed to do? Should she wait for him? Go in search of breakfast?

In the end, her craving for caffeine won out. Heading downstairs, she followed the scent of coffee.

'Ruby, my dear.'

Claudia!

She jerked to full wakefulness. 'Good morning, Mrs Keller.'

'Claudia, my dear, please. Now come into the breakfast room and have a bite to eat.'

Ignoring the foreboding that gathered in her stomach, and the far from helpful voice in her head that chanted, *You can't do this*, she squared her shoulders. Yesterday had proven that she could.

She wanted that partnership. She wanted to prove she could be ruthless when the situation warranted it. She needed to prove she wasn't a failure. Which meant she *had* to do this.

'I wasn't expecting to see you this morning.' She pasted on the blithest of smiles. 'Luis seemed to think you and Walter would be going into the office.'

'We've remote offices here at the villa as well.'

Of course they did.

'I wasn't expecting to see you up so early, after your...*adventure* last night. I trust you had a nice time.'

'Smashing, thank you.'

Really, Ruby? Smashing?

When had she ever used that word in her life before? 'Ooh, look at all this food!' She clapped her hands. 'Do you eat like this every day?'

'Not as a rule, but we wanted to spoil you and Luis today. And we didn't know what you'd prefer.'

On a sideboard stood a series of chafing dishes—exactly like the ones at posh hotels—displaying crispy strips of bacon, scrambled eggs, fried mush-rooms and hash browns. Beside them were thinly sliced cold meats and cheese, a rack of toast and a basket full of flaky pastries.

She had no hope of hiding her awe. 'It looks amazing!'

Claudia held up a coffee pot. 'Coffee?'

'Yes, please.' Grabbing a plate, she piled it with food. It seemed only polite, given all the trouble they'd gone to. Plus it gave her something to do.

Please, God, let Claudia excuse herself now.

No such luck. When Ruby took a seat at the table, Claudia took the one opposite. Her appetite promptly fled. 'You're not eating?'

'I ate earlier.'

She gave what she hoped was another blithe smile and plied herself with bacon. Her brain registered that it was seriously good—maybe the best bacon she'd ever eaten—but she couldn't enjoy it. Not with Claudia watching her like that.

If she weren't playing the role of gold-digging harpy, she'd set her cutlery down and tell Claudia that she understood her concerns about her son's hasty marriage, do all she could to ease the other woman's mind.

But she was.

So she couldn't.

Instead, she pushed food into her mouth and made 'oh-my-God-this-food-is-so-good' noises. All the while, though, her stomach churned. 'You don't have to sit with me if you've work to do, Claudia,' she finally said. 'I won't be offended. And I won't steal the family silver, I promise,' some devil made her add.

Claudia briefly closed her eyes.

'Have you seen Luis this morning? He's supposed to take me shopping. I've absolutely nothing to wear that's suitable for winter in the Alps.'

'He's with Walter in his office.'

Which probably meant he was having as much fun as she was.

'Ruby…?'

'Hmm…?' She kept her face guileless.

'You seem very…taken with my son.'

'What woman in her right mind wouldn't be?' Her laugh was genuine. 'He's handsome, generous, good company…not to mention rich.' She speared a mushroom on the end of her fork. 'It's a winning combination.'

What had Claudia hoped she'd say?

'But marriage is such a big step, my dear, and you and Luis seem to have embarked on it with very little thought.'

She abandoned the mushroom to bite into the most perfect pastry, the chewing and swallowing buying her time before she had to answer. 'Like Luis said last night. When you know, you just know. You must've felt like that when you first met Walter and—'

She broke off, wincing when she realised her faux pas.

Claudia's lips twisted. 'And we can see how well that turned out.'

Ruby dropped the pastry to her plate. 'Sorry, I didn't mean to put my foot in it.'

When Claudia pursed her lips like that, she looked so like her son it stole Ruby's breath.

Clearing her throat, Ruby pushed her plate away. 'Luis is kind. Plus he loves his parents. Those are two things that highly recommend a man. He's giving me the kind of life I want, and I mean to do everything I can to keep it. Our marriage might've been hasty, but I feel optimistic about it.' She sipped her coffee. 'I thought you'd be over the moon.'

'You did?' Claudia's voice was faint.

'He seemed to think you and his dad really wanted him to marry. I think he felt a bit pressured, sort of guilty about not living up to your expectations.'

Claudia's hand flew to her mouth.

'But you're still not happy with him, are you?' Ruby shook her head. 'Rich people! You're all so hard to please.' She smiled—a calculated, satisfied look. She'd make this woman loathe her if it was the last thing she did! 'Not Luis, though. He's not hard to please. Marrying him was like winning the jackpot.'

The stricken expression in Claudia's eyes nearly undid her.

Thankfully Luis appeared in the doorway at that moment. 'Babe!' she burbled. 'I wondered where you'd got to. You haven't forgotten about taking me shopping?'

They hadn't made any such plans, but he didn't miss a beat. 'Ready and willing whenever you say the word,' he said with admirably slavish devotion.

'Word!' Seizing her plate and cup, she set them on the sideboard before smiling at Claudia. 'See you later, Claudia.' Without waiting for a reply, she swept from the room.

'That was a mistake,' he said when they were in the car.

'You can say that again!' She wrestled with the seat belt. It kept getting stuck. She yanked harder. She wanted away from here *now*.

'Gently,' he coached, leaning across to help her. 'You simply ease it across. It's not a tug-of-war.'

He was so close that if she moved a fraction, she could touch her lips to the corner of his mouth…graze his ear with her teeth. His scent filled her lungs—an invigorating blend of pepper and mint—making her breath jam and her fingernails curl into her palms.

His gaze lifted and connected with hers and everything narrowed into this one moment. She hung there suspended between breaths, mesmerised as his gaze lowered to her lips and his eyes darkened to a brilliant sapphire. Things inside her crashed and begged and yearned.

And then he reefed back in his seat, and air rushed back into her lungs so fast it made her cough. His knuckles whitened around the steering wheel as if anchoring him in place, and something inside her started to tremble. *Ooh.* This wasn't good. It was the *opposite* of good. She needed to tread carefully around this man. She wanted a promotion, not a broken heart.

He started the car, not looking at her. 'Are you okay?'

No! But she needed to get this conversation back on track *pronto.* 'You need to make sure your mother and I aren't alone together too often.' She couldn't help that her voice wobbled. 'Because you're right—that was a *serious* mistake.'

He glanced at her, those blue eyes sharp. 'That wasn't the mistake I was referring to, but…why not?'

Because Claudia was so nice and being awful to her made her feel *really* bad. She couldn't say that out loud, though. He already felt guilty enough.

He started down the drive and she began counting the seconds until they were away from the villa, and Claudia and her Bad Ruby routine. 'She's smart and I don't want to trip up and give us away. What was the mistake you were referring to?'

'You should've left your plate on the table for the hired help to clean up.'

'That'd be rude!'

He glanced at her with a raised eyebrow, before turning out of the gates and onto the road, and she could let out the breath she'd been holding.

'Sorry. Habit.' She offered a weak smile. 'It could've been worse. If I'd known where the kitchen was, I'd have taken my dishes through and popped them in the dishwasher.'

That had him laughing, and the sound eased some of the tension that threaded through her. 'I'll give you the grand tour when we get back, but only if you promise to leave your dirty dishes on the table in future.'

'Deal.'

They were both silent for a bit. 'How did things go with your dad?'

'About as well as I expect they did for you and my mother. Didn't I think my marriage a bit rash, and was I in any kind of trouble because it wasn't like me to be so reckless blah-blah-blah?'

She grimaced. She shouldn't complain. In the general scheme of things, what Claudia and Walter thought of her didn't matter.

'What passed between you and my mother? Anything I ought to know about?'

'Same theme. Didn't I think we'd been hasty et cetera? I told her I liked you because you were good-looking and rich, and that now I had the life I wanted, there was no way I was giving it up.'

He clutched his heart as if her words were Cupid's arrow.

'I think the real low point was when I told her marrying you was like winning the jackpot.'

He grinned. 'My little *Zaubermaus*!'

She bit her lip, seeing the funny side now too. 'Thank you, Ruby.' He reached across and squeezed her hand. 'You are indeed magic. With your help, I will get to the bottom of my mother's ridiculous obsession in no time.'

Being ruthlessly awful might suck, but it was for a good cause. Luis deserved his parents' respect, and he deserved to be happy.

'No!' Ruby thrust the coat back into Luis's hands. 'It's *insanely* expensive.'

But she liked it. And he wanted her to have it.

'You're not spending that much money on me.'

Then she was going to have a pink fit later when he presented her with what he had in his pocket.

'Ruby, you need to dress the part. And as you're playing a role I've asked you to play, it's my responsibility to take care of the expenses. We agreed that in Vegas.'

'But—'

'We need to convince my parents that you're out for all you can get.'

She gnawed on her bottom lip, her eyes stormy. 'But I get to keep these, right?'

'Consider it one of those perks we discussed.'

She let out an exasperated sigh.

'Besides—' he shrugged '—the coat is cute.' It was leopard print, for heaven's sake, in some kind of mock velvet. It shouldn't work, but… 'You look adorable in it.'

Her eyes went so wide it was all he could do not to fall into them.

Clearing his throat, he shuffled back a step. 'And being leopard print probably means my mother will find it the height of bad taste.' He frowned. He was no expert on women's clothing, but nothing about that coat screamed tacky.

She silently gestured to all the other clothes he'd insisted they buy.

'I cannot have you freezing on the ski slope or when I take you sledding, or when we go to the Christmas markets.'

Her eyes widened. 'Christmas markets? *Sledding?*'

She was trying to contain her excitement and not to jump up and down like a child. She was so ridiculously easy to please it took a superhuman effort not to swoop down and kiss her.

Instead, he spread his hands wide. 'It's Christmas, sweet Ruby. We shall do Christmas things. I bet you have never been sledding, no? I think you will like it.' He loved sledding, but couldn't remember the last time he'd taken time off to enjoy such a simple pleasure. 'My parents will think I'm having a second childhood or have come down with a fever.'

That made her grin.

He leant down until they were eye level, and so close he could see the golden flecks in her irises. 'Believe me, I can afford to spend a few francs on trifles like these. I would spend a hundred times more to discover what is truly troubling my mother. Please, let us not argue about this.'

Blowing out a breath, she finally nodded. 'Okay.'

Once the items had been packaged up and dispatched by a courier, he glanced at his watch—not a Rolex. 'It's lunchtime. Where should we eat?'

'Don't look at me. I haven't a clue.'

Most women he knew would expect him to take them somewhere fancy—five-star dining in a place where they could be seen. Where could he get in last minute? He had a few favours owing and—

'Somewhere casual,' Ruby said.

He blinked.

'Somewhere I can relax and not have to be on my best behaviour. You have pubs, bars…taverns in Switzerland, right? Let's go to one of those.'

'Truly?' This woman was a miracle.

'Please tell me you know somewhere like that.'

'Of course! I will take you to my favourite place.'

What was more, they could walk.

Ten minutes later he ushered her into one of Switzerland's oldest historic bars. It was all wooden beams, stone pillars and scarred timber tables, with medieval candelabras and chandeliers casting a muted light over it all. Clasping her hands beneath her chin, Ruby turned on the spot. 'Oh, Luis…'

Had his name ever sounded sweeter? Her delight touched a chord inside him. When she'd told him a few days ago that she thought he could become one of her best friends, he hadn't known she'd return the favour.

His heart started to pound. Could he poach her for the family business? Could he convince her to remain in Switzerland? If neither her family nor her work colleagues valued her…

'I love this place *so hard.*'

'Your usual table is free, Herr Keller,' Karl, the barman, said with a smile in Ruby's direction, handing them menus.

'You have excellent taste, so I suspect this is the best seat in the house,' Ruby said as Luis ushered her towards a table in the far corner.

It made him want to laugh because very few women he knew would consider the tavern a venue worthy of praise. 'I like it, because it commands a view of the room while being out of the way enough so one can enjoy a beer and a bite to eat without being disturbed.'

She barely glanced at the menu even though it

was written in English as well as German. 'What would you recommend?'

'Are you hungry?'

One shoulder lifted. 'I had a big breakfast.' At his raised eyebrow she wrinkled her nose. 'Your mum and Ursula had obviously gone to a lot of trouble. It seemed rude not to appreciate it.'

He didn't spoil the moment by telling her she wasn't supposed to be pleasing his mother. Her consideration was so firmly ingrained it was a part of her.

He turned her menu over and pointed. 'Then I'd recommend one of the lighter meals.'

'I want something uniquely Swiss. I'm going to have fondue before going home, but that sounds a bit hearty for today. Choose me something you think I'd like.'

He ordered them both the potato pancake and brought beers back from the bar.'

'Thank you for bringing me here, Luis. I love it.'

'I am pleased to hear it.' He touched his glass to hers. 'It means I have earned some brownie points with you, yes?'

Her eyes immediately narrowed. 'Why? What have you done? Why do you need brownie points?'

'Because of this—' he gestured around '—you cannot yell at me for this.' He set the package from his pocket on the table in front of her.

While she tried her best to be *cool*, he sensed

her curiosity. Very carefully she peeled the wrapping away, opened the box… Her jaw dropped. 'You can't,' she breathed.

'I can.'

'I was only *joking*. I was trying to horrify your mother with my money-grubbing ways.'

'I know.'

'Oh, Luis, you know I can't accept this.'

She turned crestfallen eyes on him and his stomach hollowed out. 'I'm smitten, remember? You'll need to wear it for the next month, for appearances' sake. And you need to gush about it to my parents. I also want you to know that I selected it with you especially in mind.' He'd pored over the website last night when they'd returned from dancing. Because he still couldn't sleep. It had been couriered first thing this morning. 'I thought you would like it.'

'It's the most beautiful watch I've ever seen in my life. But a Rolex…?'

'Let's try it on and see how it fits.' With one fluid motion he had the watch out of the box and clasped around her left wrist. 'See? It suits you.'

Unlike the watch, her stunned expression was priceless. 'I still can't—'

'If you're truly uncomfortable accepting this, then obviously you can return it to me. But I'm very much hoping that you will keep it as a memento of your time here in Switzerland.'

'Along with the clothes and whatever else you

deem necessary,' she murmured. Her gaze returned to his, oddly earnest. 'I will be returning this to you—and I'm not going to ask how much it cost or I'll be so worried about damaging or losing it that I'd never breathe properly again—but I want you to know it's a real thrill to wear it.' She touched it reverently. 'Thank you.'

He couldn't explain why, but her simple sincerity had a lump lodging in his throat. Clearing it, he said, 'Enough of that. I've been meaning to ask you how your conversation with your parents went yesterday afternoon.' There had been no time to ask prior to dinner, and afterwards they'd danced rather than talked.

She leaned across the table towards him. 'Do you know what I did?'

Her scent wrapped around him and he dragged a grateful breath into starved lungs. She smelled of an intoxicating mixture of spun sugar and sun-warmed pears. 'What did you do?'

'I channelled some of the attitude I've developed here. And I suddenly realised that the inspiration for my Bad Ruby persona was…'

'Christa?'

'Yes! How did you know?'

'Lucky guess.'

Shaking her head, she picked up her beer. 'It…'

'What?'

'It's going to sound odd, but it made me feel a whole lot better about myself. I've spent so long envying Christa that I never really stopped to consider…' She set her beer down without taking a sip. 'I want what she has—the trappings of success, the good opinion of others…my parents' unconditional love.'

The way she whispered that last bit had something in his chest twisting.

'But I don't want to be *like* her. I don't want to be the person I pretend to be when I'm around your parents. It was a bit of a revelation, frankly, and it's helped me make peace with it all somehow.'

He stared at her, stunned.

'Meeting you and coming here to Switzerland has been good for me.' She suddenly grinned. 'Of course, they were totally appalled at my rash marriage, and the fact I won't be home for Christmas. How could I do that to them? What was I thinking? You know the drill. I sent them a picture of us at our fake wedding, and told them who you were and how successful you are—' She glanced up. 'I hope you don't mind?'

'Not in the least.' A weight settled on his shoulders.

'When I sent them a picture of the villa, I swear to God they were silent for a full minute.' She happy-sighed. 'I couldn't believe how freeing it was not to worry what they thought of me.'

'Good for you.'

'Maybe you were right. Maybe I've been teaching people to treat me like a doormat.'

He rubbed a hand over his face. *Damn.*

Their food arrived, but Ruby didn't reach for her cutlery. Instead, she surveyed him. 'Out with it.'

She saw too much. But… 'Neither one of us needs much of an imagination to know what they're going to say when we divorce.' This charade he'd talked her into might have provided her with ammunition to sock it to her family now, but it would also give them ample ammunition once she returned to Australia. *Alone.* His hands clenched as he imagined their 'I told you so's'. They'd try and make her feel small again.

Her face fell and he felt like a heel. He should've let her enjoy the moment while she could. Pushing his shoulders back, he stabbed a finger to the table. 'But you will have the promotion to boast about. And you know you *don't* want to act like Christa to get the things you want. A revelation like that is gold.'

She straightened.

'And if you realise you've been letting people take advantage of you…'

She nodded. 'Then I can take steps to stop it.'

'What kind of steps?'

She lifted her cutlery with a shrug. 'I've got the best part of a month to come up with a plan. Now tell me about all of these Christmas events you mentioned earlier.'

CHAPTER FIVE

'RUBY, I'VE BEEN hoping to find an opportunity to talk to you since breakfast.'

Oh, God.

They'd not taken three steps inside the villa before Claudia appeared on the landing above. Ruby wanted to latch onto Luis's arm and hold on for dear life, but...

Actually, under the guise of Bad Ruby, that was a perfectly legitimate reaction. Seizing his arm, she pulled him close. And relished the warm muscled strength beneath her fingertips.

Don't stroke him.

Oh, for heaven's sake, a tiny brush of her fingers up and down that arm wouldn't hurt. She had to be convincing here. This was his *mother* they were trying to deceive.

Don't dig your fingernails into his biceps to test how strong it is.

Why not? It was just part of the charade. And she *was* only human.

The tensile strength of Luis's arm, his heat and

tall broad bulk—his sheer masculinity—swamped her senses and her head reeled. *This* was why she shouldn't touch him. Desire and need lit through her veins like wildfire. Their amazing night of lovemaking rose in her mind and with every atom of her being she ached to repeat it. Just one more time—

Nostrils flaring, she snapped that thought off.

Latching onto Luis might not have been the best idea she'd had all day, but it was a mistake she could fix. Straightening, she released him and smoothed a hand down the front of her shirt, but her fingertips continued to throb. It was as if the man had got into her bloodstream. Like alcohol.

She needed to start being more careful. She trusted Luis—it felt as if they were already the best of friends. But she couldn't trust him with her heart. He'd told her he wouldn't fall in love with her, and she believed him.

Lifting her chin, she glanced in Claudia's direction, but didn't meet her eyes. 'You want to speak to me? *Again?*' She wished she found being unfriendly easier.

Claudia flew down the last few steps to seize Ruby's hands. 'That's the thing, my dear. I feel I gave you the wrong impression at breakfast and I wanted to apologise.'

She wanted to *what*?

Claudia squeezed her hands, her face earnest.

'I'm mortified if you thought I was being disapproving. I want to assure you I wasn't.'

She assumed an injured expression and glanced away. 'You hurt my feelings.'

Dear God, how could she be such a convincing cow? Claudia ought to kick her out into the cold, cold snow and tell Luis to wake up to himself.

The pressure on her hands increased. 'It's just…it's very hard sometimes for a mother to loosen her apron strings.'

She turned back with a frown. Something in Claudia's voice… Luis was right. Something deeper was going on here.

'All Walter and I want is for Luis to be happy.'

'You clearly don't think *I* can make him happy.'

'That's not what I meant at all.' She swung to her son. 'Tell her, Luis. Tell her how I'm not good with surprises, and that it takes me a while to adjust to change.'

One broad shoulder lifted. 'It's true.'

'We were so very surprised by your announcement yesterday. It took us off guard, and I've yet to adjust.'

Ruby stuck her nose in the air. 'Would it be easier if we gave you the room to do that? Luis and I could move into the apartment in Zurich.'

'No!' Claudia looked utterly horrified. 'Besides, it's tiny and not suitable for—'

'We could buy another bigger apartment, couldn't we?' Ruby swung to Luis, clapping her hands and bouncing on the balls of her feet. 'Or you could buy me that yacht you promised and we could sail the French Riviera or the Costa del Sol or somewhere ridiculously exotic. What do you think? That could be fun.'

'That's more a summer activity.' Luis glared at his mother. 'But, Mutti, if you'd rather we—'

'Absolutely not!' Panic raced across her mother-in-law's face. 'I want you both here for Christmas. I want us to become a family. Oh, Ruby, I want you to understand you are truly welcome here. That's why I've been waiting for you.'

Oh, God! Claudia's guilt and concern were so real—

Closing her eyes, Ruby brought to mind her conversation with Luis last night, the way his eyes had dimmed when he'd spoken of his parents. He clearly felt confused and hurt, but rather than stewing in resentment he was worried about *them*. He deserved to get to the bottom of this— whatever this was.

Opening her eyes, she pushed her shoulders back. A good leader dealt with conflict and didn't shy away from confrontation.

'We really are delighted to welcome you to the family, Ruby, and as you said this morning— you've every right to feel optimistic about your marriage. From now on, I plan to be optimistic too.'

Was she *serious*?

'And to prove I mean what I say, I have something for you.'

Taking her arm, Claudia led her into the blue drawing room and across to a table holding an ornate ormolu box that she'd have sworn wasn't there last night. Behind her, Luis's quick intake of breath told her something momentous was about to happen.

Lifting the lid, Claudia reached inside to pull out a vintage velvet box. 'I'd like you to have this.'

A fist tightened about Ruby's chest and squeezed until she could barely breathe. The shape of the box told her that this was going to be a piece of jewellery. A significant piece of jewellery.

No, no, no.

'I noticed you're not wearing an engagement ring.'

She managed to force out a giggle without hyperventilating. 'Well, we kind of skipped that part.'

'This ring was my great-grandmother's. It's quite the statement piece. I had it thoroughly cleaned and inspected earlier in the year.'

When she'd decided Luis must marry?

Please share your reasons, Claudia, so we can end this awful farce.

Claudia didn't of course. What she did was pull the ring from its velvet casing and hold it up for Ruby's inspection. 'Do you like it?'

Her breath caught. The ring was the most beautiful thing Ruby had ever seen. Art deco in design, it consisted of a row of needle baguette-cut diamonds graded in size—a long one in the middle and then descending in size on either side.

'Mutti…' Luis breathed.

That pulled her out of her trance. Glancing at him, she hoped for some clue as to how to play this, but he was staring at the ring and his mother with such a lost look in his eyes it made her chest ache.

She toyed briefly with the notion of saying she didn't want a hand-me-down ring, that Luis had promised to buy her a brand-new one. Though he'd already spent a small fortune. Her fingers brushed the watch on her wrist. She couldn't put him to further expense.

Swallowing, and internally wincing and cringing and dying a thousand deaths, she took the ring and put it on her finger and they all stared at it. 'It's the most beautiful ring I've ever seen,' she said. She'd wanted her voice to be loud and discordant, brash, but it emerged as little more than a breathy whisper.

Get with the programme, Ruby!

Holding her hand at arm's length, she admired the ring from every conceivable angle. 'It must be worth an absolute fortune.'

Both Luis and his mother's heads rocked back.

Bouncing across, she hugged Claudia. 'Thank you! Thank you! Thank you!' Easing away, she held her hand out at arm's length again, angling it this way and that. 'Look how it catches the light. I'm going to be the envy of every woman I meet. Now I'm really starting to feel a part of the family.' She beamed at her mother-in-law. 'Best apology ever! Please offend me again soon if this is the outcome.'

Claudia's smile grew strained, and Luis winced, but she couldn't take pity on him. He *needed* her to be awful. Snuggling into his side, she held her hand up. 'Isn't it beautiful, babe?'

He smiled valiantly. 'Not as beautiful as you, my little *Zaubermaus*.'

She saw the moment Claudia's gaze landed on the Rolex, and increased her smile's wattage. 'Pretty, isn't it? I've been quite the lucky girl today.'

'So it would seem,' Claudia said faintly. With a shake of her head, she clapped her hands and straightened. 'What do the two of you have planned for the rest of the day?'

'Luis has promised me a tour of the house.'

'How wonderful. Do let me tag along. I know a lot of the history.'

All Ruby wanted to do was curl up in a ball and sleep for a week.

Claudia took one of her arms and turned her towards the grand hall and its staircase. 'And what do you have planned for tomorrow?'

Luis took Ruby's other arm. 'Why?'

'Your father and I thought it'd be fun if the four of us went skiing.'

He gaped at her.

'Why are you looking at me like that, Luis? It's not unknown for your father and I to take time off work. We figured we'd have a bit of a holiday too. Get to know Ruby.'

Bad. Worse. Hell. Handbasket.

Her gaze narrowed. They'd find a way to turn it to their advantage.

Claudia squeezed her arm. 'Have you ever been skiing, Ruby?'

'Never once in my whole entire life.'

'Would you like to try? It's not roller skating, I know, but I think you'll enjoy it.'

She made a show of admiring her ring again to stop from bursting into hysterical laughter. 'This is insured, isn't it?'

'Absolutely. And the skiing, Ruby?'

'Oh, I couldn't imagine anything I'd rather do.' She beamed at her mother-in-law then up at Luis. 'Babe? What do you think?'

'Whatever you want, sweetheart, whatever you want.'

'Now the house,' Claudia said with relish.

Forty minutes later, Luis pointed at Ruby and mimed yawning behind his mother's back.

Covering her mouth, she feigned an enormous yawn.

Claudia swung around from identifying the faces in a series of paintings along one of the long galleries. 'Have I worn you out, Ruby?'

'Sorry, Claudia, this is all fascinating.' Actually, it really was. 'But I don't think I've adjusted to the time zone yet.'

'Why don't you have a lie-down before dinner?'

'That's an excellent idea. It's been such an exciting day.' She played with her watch and admired her ring again, so the other woman couldn't possibly misinterpret what it was that had made the day so exciting in Ruby's eyes.

Luis placed an idle arm across her shoulders. 'I'll come with you—'

'No, no.' She slipped from beneath his arm. 'Spend some time with your mother.' She hoped he could read the message in her eyes—*Find out why she wanted you to marry!* The sooner he started peck-pecking away at that, the better. 'I know the way back to our suite.'

Before he could argue, she turned and fled. As soon as she was out of sight, she slumped. Dear God, this was only Day Two. How was she going to last an entire month?

Ruby leaped off the sofa the moment Luis entered their suite an hour later. He blinked and halted. He'd thought she'd be napping in the other room.

'Did you find anything out? Did you get any clues as to why your mother wanted you to marry?'

A weight slammed down on his shoulders. 'All I could get out of her was that she's looking forward to getting to know and love you like a daughter.'

'Oh, that's so not good.' Ruby paced back and forth in front of the fireplace, wringing her hands. 'How much awfuller do I have to be?'

He fell down to the sofa.

'She's so determined to find the heart of gold beneath all of this trashy surface glitter.'

Her analogy had him wincing.

'I have to somehow convince her that her optimism is misplaced. We have to work out a way to do that asap, Luis. The longer she goes on thinking I'm *redeemable*, the—'

She broke off to wring her hands again.

He straightened. 'What?'

'You want to get to the heart of the problem. You don't actually want to hurt her.'

'She won't be hurt!' He shot to his feet. 'She'll be disappointed. There's a difference.'

She thrust her hand up, pointed to *that* ring. 'She can't keep giving me jewellery!'

Her outrage made him laugh. 'I thought you loved it,' he teased, dropping back down to the sofa.

'It's the second most beautiful ring I've ever seen.' She sent him a weak smile. 'After my wedding ring.'

She was *so* keeping that at the end of all this.

'Wearing it terrifies me.' She fell down beside him. 'What if I lose it?'

'You won't lose it.'

'What if I break it?'

'You won't break it.'

'You do know you're getting this back when we're done? I'm not planning to abscond with it or anything.'

Reaching out, he closed his hand around hers. 'Despite the consummate acting, I know you're not here for the money.'

Cloudy hazel eyes met his. 'Why were you so surprised that she gave it to me?'

Lifting her hand, he brushed his thumb across the ring. It was a significant piece in the family collection and worth an absolute fortune. He didn't tell Ruby that, though. He didn't want to make her even more nervous. The ring suited her. He enjoyed seeing it on her finger. 'Of all the family pieces, this ring is my mother's favourite. On special occasions, she wears it as a dress ring.'

A low tortured sound left her throat.

'In giving it to you, she's letting me know that she accepts my choice and is determined to love you.'

'Clearly we need to nip *that* in the bud.'

Nodding, he lifted her hand to his lips and pressed a kiss to the knuckle just above where the ring sat. The satin softness of her skin and her warm pear scent had his heart suddenly thudding.

Her hand trembled in his, and a thrill shook him. If he—

Tugging her hand from his, she shot away to cram herself into the corner of the sofa, and his pulse thundered in his ears. *Verdammt*. What was he doing? He hadn't meant…

Ruby rubbed at her hand as if to rub his touch away. She felt it too, this insistent heat that threatened to become an inferno from the smallest of touches. If he reached for her now, would she let him—?

No. Ruby didn't want any romantic complications, and he couldn't think of anything he wanted less! He had no desire to hurt her. After everything she was doing for him, he wanted to make her life easier, not harder.

She shot to her feet. 'I think I might go and take that nap now.' And still she didn't look at him.

'And while I'm doing that, you need to put your thinking cap on and come up with some new and novel ways for me to alienate your parents.'

Disappearing into the bedroom, she closed the door behind her. He reached up to loosen his collar only to find he wasn't wearing one.

Ruby landed on her rear for the fourth time in three minutes. Her eyes danced as Luis helped her to her feet. 'Despite appearances otherwise, I'm having a ball.'

Anyone with eyes in their head could see how much fun Ruby was having. 'Angle your skis like this.'

They made it down the rest of the beginners' slope without incident.

'When will I be good enough to go up there?' She pointed to a chair lift that moved towards one of the more demanding upper slopes.

'Well, considering you're a natural…'

Her jaw dropped.

'Why so surprised?' he demanded.

'I've never been a natural at anything before.'

'Not even roller skating?'

That had her laughing again. 'Well, besides that.'

He frowned. What about the law? Didn't she feel a natural affinity for her chosen vocation? He stared at her for a long moment before pointing up the *very* gentle slope. 'Once more down here. Do everything I tell you.'

She followed his every instruction. Turned right when he ordered her to, and then left, increased her speed, halted quickly—all without falling over once.

'See? You've mastered the basics. You're a natural.' He glanced at the slopes and then back at her. 'How do you feel about tackling the T-bar lift and trying something a little more advanced?'

Her face lit up. Grinding his molars together, he tried to stamp out the hunger that rose through him. He needed to keep things normal between them. Or if not normal, at least not uncomfortable.

He'd agreed to the no-sex rule. He *would* keep his word.

Instead of hauling her into his arms and kissing her, he concentrated on helping her negotiate the T-bar and teaching her to ski.

She fell. Of course, she did. But the exercise made her eyes bright and her cheeks pink, and she looked utterly adorable in her powder-blue ski suit, and her fuzzy pink beanie.

He hadn't expected to enjoy himself so much. He'd thought he'd be impatient to get out on the more advanced runs. But watching Ruby get the hang of skiing, witnessing her delight and growing confidence, gave him a warm glow that was ten times more potent than hurtling down the side of a mountain. And watching her was a pleasurable torment he had no desire to forgo.

'Oh, please, can we do that again?' she demanded when they reached the bottom.

Without a word, he led her back over to the T-bar. 'What made you decide to study law?' he asked when they were halfway up the slope. He might not be able to kiss her, but he could indulge his curiosity about her and her life.

Her swift glance told him his question had surprised her. 'When we get to the top,' she murmured. 'I need to concentrate on not falling off this thing and causing a pile-up.'

He chuckled. 'I would not let that happen to you, sweet Ruby.'

She dragged in a breath, sent him another glance. 'I think you have to stop calling me that.'

It was he who suddenly needed to concentrate on his balance. When they reached the top, he took her arm and they skied a little off to the side. 'Why?' he demanded. The day was crisp and clear, the snow powder soft beneath their skis, and the sky blue above. And she was *sweet*!

'Because my little *Zaubermaus* is much more in character for this charade of ours.'

She didn't look at him as she spoke, and his frown deepened. 'Where is the harm when nobody can overhear?'

She turned to face him. 'We're *friends*, Luis, nothing more. *Sweet Ruby* is something a lover would call me, not a friend.'

He opened his mouth to argue, then closed it and drew himself up to his full height. 'Very well.'

'And now you're offended.'

'Am not,' he said through gritted teeth. He gestured for her to set off down the slope before him. 'Now tell me what inspired your decision to study law.'

'It's not very original.' She kept her gaze on the slope in front of her. 'But as soon as I finished the book *To Kill A Mockingbird*, I wanted to be just like Atticus Finch.'

'You wished to become a criminal defence attorney?'

'I was thirteen at the time, Luis, I didn't understand the different permutations of the law. As I became older and wiser, certain people pointed out that I wasn't the best of debaters and that maybe I'd prefer something a little...gentler than criminal law.'

'Your family are pigs.'

She started, swerved and face-planted into a snow drift. Rolling to her back, she half laughed, half glared. 'Next time, warn me before you say something like that.'

He crouched down beside her. 'Why did you let them belittle you and your dreams? Why did you not stand up for yourself?'

Her laughter drained away. 'Some of us aren't as lucky in our families as you are, Luis. You try being put down for most of your life and see how long your confidence lasts.'

Swearing under his breath, he hauled her upright, his hands curling around her upper arms to help her find purchase on the snow. 'You are smart and talented. *That's* what you should believe.'

Her gaze collided with his, her eyes becoming suspiciously bright. She wobbled, her hands landing against his chest for balance, her ski sticks dangling uselessly from her wrists and bumping against them both gently, and the air charged *just like that*.

What would she do if he hauled her against him and kissed her, as deeply and thoroughly as he ached to? Her eyes widened and her lips parted, as if she'd read that thought in his face... She edged closer as if she couldn't help it, her breath sawing in and out of her lungs, and everything inside him clenched, leaving him nothing more than a swirling, seething mass of need. He dipped his head towards hers—

With a sound midway between a growl and a groan, she pushed away.

He dropped his arms immediately. *Verdammt!* What was he thinking? Closing his eyes, he tried to quieten the racing of his heart.

'Parents at ten o'clock,' she murmured.

Bracing himself, he opened his eyes. 'I don't like to ask this of you, but can you pretend to hate skiing?'

Startled eyes met his and he grimaced. 'It's one of their favourite pastimes, and if you hate it...'

'Got it.'

She dusted herself off, just as his parents came to a halt beside them.

'It is the perfect day for skiing,' Walter said, beaming at Ruby. 'You are lucky. Is it not invigorating up here on the mountain?'

She sniffed. 'It's certainly cold.'

Not as cold as Ruby's voice, though. Which was positively frigid. It was the kind of voice Luis would like to hear her use on Howard and Hugh. And her family.

Walter blinked, but recovered beautifully. 'We've

been keeping an eye out for you both. Ruby, you're a natural.'

Verdammt. His father's warmth could melt polar icecaps.

Luis slung an arm around Ruby's shoulders. 'She's brilliant at everything.'

'Yes, yes.' Ruby waved that away, pushing Luis's arm off her shoulders. 'But I've had enough for the moment.'

Walter's smile froze.

'I'm tired of falling over, of being cold and having to deal with all of this...*snow.* I know you'll excuse me while I make my way to the ski lodge to warm my frozen bones.'

Her sulky expression suddenly transformed and she beamed at them. 'I'm hoping I might spot a celebrity or two. Luis says it's not outside the realms of possibility. So that's the rest of my day sorted. You'll know where to find me when you're done.'

With that, she made her way down the hill in the direction of the ski lodge. Luis watched her go, his heart heavy. She'd been having such a good time.

Until you spoiled it by nearly kissing her!

Still, couldn't he have found another way—?

Stop it!

Ruby would be the first to tell him she wasn't here to have fun.

'Shouldn't you go with her?' Claudia finally

said, and that was when he realised how the silence on their tiny bit of the mountain burned. He turned. Why wouldn't they confide in him?

'Ruby is wonderful and adorable, but she sometimes has a short attention span. She'll have a hot chocolate, warm up, and then she'll be ready to give the slopes another chance.'

Walter shook his head. 'I'm not so sure about that, son. She didn't seem at all impressed with the mountain so far.'

'She'll come around.' He spoke blithely, confidently, as if he couldn't understand there being any other alternative, pretending not to see the glance his parents exchanged. 'I love what Ruby loves and she'll learn to love what I love too. Isn't that what marriage is all about?'

If he continued to play the blind fool, surely they'd become so worried about him one of them would crack.

'You haven't spent much time with Ruby so far, Vati,' he shot at his father.

Walter started. 'I've been busy.'

With what? His father was sixty-three and still cut a fine figure, but over the last eight months he'd reduced the number of hours he worked, claiming he wanted to start enjoying more leisure time.

His mind ticked over. Was that what was behind this desire to see him married? Did his parents want to see him settled before he became

CEO of Keller Enterprises? 'I'm sorry if my impromptu honeymoon has meant you've had to cover for me.'

'It's done nothing of the sort,' Claudia said in a crisp no-nonsense tone. 'As we've told you before, Luis. If you do not wish to be CEO of Keller Enterprises, you do not have to be. We would never push that responsibility onto you. We're more than happy for you to continue heading up your own division.'

So whatever the problem was, it was nothing to do with work, then.

'Son, let me assure you I do have plans to get to know Ruby much better.' His father patted his shoulder. 'Starting this evening.'

Before he could ask what on earth that meant, his parents had set off down the slope. Settling his goggles over his eyes, he followed at a slower pace. Ruby was right. This wasn't going to plan. They needed to change tactics. He'd thought spreading the shocks out over the course of the month would be the better strategy.

Not now. Now they were going in with the heavy artillery.

CHAPTER SIX

SIPPING HOT CHOCOLATE, and flicking through a discarded magazine, Ruby did her best not to cast too many wistful glances out of the window at all the skiers zipping down the slopes. Okay, well, maybe not all of them were zipping. Some, like her, were falling flat on their faces. But they still looked as if they were having a great time.

She'd briefly considered sneaking back out to the beginners' slope just to practise the techniques Luis had taught her, but she'd knocked that idea on its head as soon as she'd had it. What if Walter or Claudia should see? Luis had said he wanted them to think she hated skiing.

She couldn't give them any reason to believe otherwise. She needed them to start believing her an utter nightmare. If they thought her the kind of woman who'd make their son's life miserable, it'd spur them to action.

Disappointing her own family had come easily enough. It shouldn't be that hard to do the same with Luis's.

Except his were lovely and—

Stop! If she wasn't careful, she'd start imagining what it'd be like to have them for her parents and that wouldn't do. It wouldn't do at all.

Besides, after nearly tossing all caution to the wind and throwing herself into Luis's arms up there on the mountain, they needed a serious timeout from one another. What on earth had she been thinking?

Wincing, she gritted her teeth. Clearly she hadn't been thinking. It was just…he'd said such lovely things to her. And seemed to believe them.

It didn't mean anything.

Of course it didn't mean anything!

Thank God she'd come to her senses in time. Neither of them wanted the complications a physical relationship would bring. She didn't want a broken heart, and he didn't want to break it. Why was that so hard to remember?

Enough. Glancing around for distraction, her gaze landed on a little girl on the outskirts of a nearby group who clutched a doll in one hand and some doll's clothes in the other. She couldn't be older than five or six. 'Mama—' She tugged on a woman's sleeve. 'Mama, can you help—?'

'For heaven's sake, Philomena! Can't you play by yourself for five seconds without interrupting me? I'm having an important discussion with your aunts. I don't want to hear another peep from you.'

The child's shoulders slumped and she edged away to sit on a nearby chair, head bent over her doll.

Oh, God. She knew exactly what that felt like. Being ignored. Being scolded. Feeling invisible. Swallowing, she rubbed a hand across her chest, before leaning across and catching the little girl's eye. 'What's your dolly's name?'

Biting her lip, the little girl glanced at her mother, and then slid off her chair and edged across. 'Jessica Barbara Lillian Gosland.'

'Heavens, that's an impressive name. I'm just plain old Ruby.'

Philomena chewed her lip and then leaned closer. 'She's Jessica Barbara Lillian *Ruby* Gosland.'

Ruby feigned delight. 'What a perfect name! And I can see that she has quite the enviable wardrobe.'

'Do you want to see?'

'More than life itself.' Playing doll dress-ups might not be as much fun as skiing, but it was fun all the same.

She didn't know how long she and Philomena played for. At one point her mother turned to Ruby and said, 'If she's bothering you…'

'Not at all,' Ruby assured her.

She ordered three hot chocolates—one for her, one for Phil, and one for Jessica Barbara Lillian *Ruby* Gosland. They ate hot chips while making up places and events to wear all of those lovely clothes. They had a ball.

'We see you've found a friend.'

Ruby swung around to find Claudia beaming at her. Walter smiled too, but Luis… She swallowed. Luis had closed his eyes on a grimace.

With a superhuman effort, she pasted on a smile. 'This is Philomena and this is Jessica Barbara Lillian Ruby Gosland—' when she held up the doll, she couldn't work out whether Luis wanted to laugh or groan '—who loves clothes almost as much as I do.'

'We're going to a very fancy party,' Phil said. 'What's it called again, Ruby?'

'A film premiere. We have to look fabulous and glamorous and dazzle everyone we see.'

'And eat cake and drink fizzy drink.'

'And drip with diamonds.' Oh, God, this so wasn't the message she ought to be giving a little girl. 'And then we'll have a slumber party and eat more cake and have the best fun, right, Phil?'

Phil's mother chose that moment to push inside their cosy circle. She smiled flirtatiously at Luis, who immediately placed both hands on Ruby's shoulders as if afraid the woman might eat him alive. With a shrug, she gestured to her daughter. 'Come along, Philomena. It's time to stop bothering the nice lady.'

'She was no bother at all.' To Phil she said, 'Thank you for letting me play with your doll and all of those beautiful clothes.'

'I had fun,' Phil whispered.

'Me too,' she whispered back.

It didn't matter how much Luis glared and grimaced, she couldn't cold-shoulder the child. She just *couldn't*. She kept waving at the little girl until she'd disappeared.

Claudia sat across from her, literally beaming. 'You like children?'

Luis sat beside her and kicked her ankle. It wasn't hard, but there was an edge to his posture, and she knew exactly what he wanted from her.

'Not particularly.' She tossed her head. 'The man who was with them when they first walked in looked like Daniel Radcliffe—you know, the actor who played Harry Potter—and I thought I might get a chance to meet him if I played with the little girl.'

Claudia and Walter stared at her as if they had no idea what to say. She didn't blame them.

She turned to Luis. 'That doll had the most divine dress. I took a photo. I want one just like it.'

He nodded. 'I'm sure that can be managed.'

'I don't believe you.' Claudia slapped a hand to the table. 'You were so good with that little girl. You built a rapport with her. It was a delight to witness. You don't need to feel ashamed of that.'

Claudia was too astute and far too perceptive. Shrugging, Ruby tried a different tack. 'She was clearly feeling neglected and as I was too…' She let the sentence trail away with an injured sniff, hoping that'd be the end of it.

Claudia shook her head. 'One day, you will make a wonderful mother, Ruby.'

'Good Lord! I'm not the least interested in *having* children. I told Luis that before we married.' She suddenly frowned. 'I did tell you that, babe, didn't I?'

His eyes widened. He ran a finger around his collar. 'You did?'

'Absolutely. Don't you remember?'

'I…uh…' He lifted a shoulder. 'No matter, sweetheart. If you don't want children, we don't have to have them.'

Both Walter and Claudia leaned towards him. 'Are you serious?' Walter said.

At the same time as Claudia said, 'What, *never*?'

It wasn't just shock that raced across their features. It was panic. They stared at each other stricken, and for a moment she thought Walter was going to pull Claudia into his arms. With the smallest shake of her head, though, Claudia gave him a bravely game smile that pierced Ruby's heart and made it ache.

'You can't mean that,' Claudia said gently.

'Why not? Just because a woman doesn't want children doesn't make her unnatural, you know?'

Claudia sat back as if slapped. 'Of course it doesn't. It's just…'

She raised an eyebrow. 'Yes?'

'It's just,' Walter leaped in, 'that children are

such a blessing. And it was clear you were enjoying the company of your little friend.'

'There's a huge difference between playing with a child for half an hour and raising one. Being a cool honorary aunt is the role I see for myself. Motherhood? No, thank you.'

Claudia reached across the table to grip Ruby's hand. 'It can be a joy, though.'

What on earth was she supposed to say to all this? Beneath the table, she kicked Luis's foot.

He straightened. 'It's Ruby's decision, Mutti.'

'Darling…' Claudia frowned. 'It's your decision too.'

He shrugged. 'I never figured children would be part of my future.'

Her mouth opened and closed and then she folded her arms. 'You never thought marriage would feature in your future either, and look what happened.'

He beamed at her and then at Ruby, slipping an arm around Ruby's shoulders. 'Yep, Ruby came along and knocked me off my feet. That's enough of a blessing for me.'

The smile is fake. The words are fake.

It didn't matter how much Ruby told herself that, though. When Luis looked at her as if he'd like to eat her up for dessert, she melted.

'Did you see the look on your mother's face when I said we wouldn't be having children?' Ruby dropped to the sofa, her chest burning. 'It was as if I'd stabbed her through the heart.'

Luis muttered a curse, closing the door to their suite with the softest of snicks. 'Why were you playing with that little girl anyway? What were you thinking?'

'I didn't know you were all suddenly going to descend on me! I thought you'd be hours yet. Why didn't you text me to tell me you were on your way? I'd have made sure to clear the decks and look suitably bored and unimpressed.'

'Sorry, sorry!' He scrubbed both hands back through his hair. 'That wasn't fair.'

She twisted her wedding ring around and around. 'She was so lonely, Luis. It was awful the way the adults were ignoring her.'

He eased down beside her, reached out and squeezed her hand. 'So you played with her and cheered her up.'

A moment ago, the sofa had felt generously large, but when Luis sat on it, it shrank. His scent drenched the air, making it hard to think straight. She did her best to ease away without being obvious. 'I wouldn't have if I'd known you'd all catch me in the act.'

'Really?'

She went to say of course not, but the words wouldn't come.

'Ah, sweet Ru—'

He broke off with a cough. 'You have a soft heart,' he said instead.

Her heart hammered in her throat. She ignored it. 'We don't need your parents knowing that, though. They have to start hating me soon. I'm a nightmare! A total spoiled brat and—okay, okay.' She raised her hands when he opened his mouth to interrupt. 'Not hate, but they have to see how unsuitable I am.'

'You'd think so, but...'

'For your sake, they're determined to make a connection with me.' She blew out a breath. 'They love you a lot.'

He nodded heavily.

Why did he wear that love like a burden? Because he'd made a habit out of putting their needs before his own? She glanced at him. 'They love each other a lot too.'

He shrugged. 'Like I said, they're best friends.'

She wasn't so sure. At the ski lodge, she'd formed the distinct impression that Walter and Claudia were more than best friends, and that they were still very much in love with each other. Not that she had any intention of voicing such an opinion. At least, not before she was sure of it. But if they were, then why were they *just* best friends?

And she'd thought *her* family was complicated!

'Do you ever wish you'd become a criminal lawyer?'

The abrupt change of topic threw her. 'I...'

'Your initial interest in the law was sparked by an altruistic impulse and I wondered if that's what kept the dream alive. Or if it was something more prosaic.'

Those blue eyes stared at her with such intensity, her mouth dried. 'Honestly?'

His gaze sharpened. 'Yes.'

'If I tell you the truth, can I then ask you a personal question?'

'Yes.'

He didn't hesitate and it made her smile.

He laughed then, his eyes briefly dancing. 'We're married, Ruby. You can ask me anything you want.'

Oh, she was going to miss him when this was over.

'So…?' he prompted.

'I can't tell you how many times I've read *To Kill A Mockingbird*, but it's been at least once a year since I was thirteen, and I've watched the old black and white movie with Gregory Peck more times than I can count too. The first time I read it—' she shook her head '—it destroyed me. I couldn't believe justice wasn't done. I cried. Not just as I read the story, but for days afterwards whenever I thought about it.'

He nodded as if her reaction made perfect sense.

'And it's not that my family mocked me, but they did dismiss it as *just a book*—just a work of fiction. But the thing is, injustice does exist in the world. And right doesn't always win over wrong. But the more I read the book, the more I realised that it's the fight that's important. Atticus knows he's not going to win, but he gives it his best anyway. Because it deserves his best. And that's what I wanted to do when I was a teenager. I wanted to give my best in the fight against injustice.'

'What changed?'

She stared at her hands, her lips twisting. 'You mean why did I end up working for a firm that specialises in business law and contract negotiations?'

'Yes.'

Resting her head back against the sofa, she stared at the ceiling. Dark beams ran its length—solid and comforting in their timelessness, the deep wood gleaming in the soft light. She frowned. Why *hadn't* her dreams lasted, in the same way that old timber had lasted? Why had she given them up?

Her stomach churned. 'Christa.'

'Ruby—'

She held up a hand to cut him off. 'I should explain a bit more about Horrid Cousin Christa, because there's every chance I'm being unfair to her.'

'I find that hard to believe.'

Mirroring her position, so that he too stared up at the ceiling, he took her hand in his. His touch felt somehow solid, though, and as eternal as the beams above them, anchoring her to this room and the here and now.

'When I was ten and Christa eleven, her parents were killed in a car accident. It was awful. My mother had been close to her sister—Christa's mum—and was devastated. Christa came to live with us.'

His hand tightened about hers.

'Initially I was excited about that. Not that she'd lost her parents, you understand? I couldn't imagine anything worse. But she was my cousin and I adored her. I wanted us to be sisters.'

'It didn't work out that way?'

She shook her head. 'At ten, I had no hope of understanding how troubled she was. And initially she took all of my parents' time and attention. And while it left me a bit forlorn, I knew it was also only fair.'

'Oh, Ruby.'

'But the thing is, Luis—' she turned her head on the cushion to meet his gaze '—from that moment on she never gave any of it back. She continued to monopolise their time and attention.' Their love. 'I tried talking to her when I was fourteen and she was fifteen. And you know what she said? That she wasn't losing another family and that she was taking everything that was mine so I'd know how she'd felt. I tried talking to my parents but they told me to stop being selfish. And when Christa went to them with lies about my behaviour towards her...' Her throat thickened and her eyes blurred. Even after all this time that injustice still hurt. 'Well, they took her side.'

'I'm sorry.'

His warmth had her eyes burning. 'It not only felt like she'd stolen them from me. It felt like they'd wanted to be stolen. I know in part they just felt so bad for her that they...'

'Overcompensated?'

She nodded. 'But since then, I feel as if I've been locked in some kind of battle to win back their love and maybe best her somehow.'

'And instead of following your dream, you found yourself chasing higher salaries and higher-status jobs to prove that you were just as good as Christa.'

Staring at the palms of her hands, she frowned. 'Yeah.'

He didn't say anything. He didn't have to. *What* had she been thinking?

'It's not healthy, is it?'

'No.'

'No,' she agreed, slowly straightening. 'I think we can safely say that's what's commonly defined as a toxic relationship.'

The only thing that competing with Christa had accomplished was to satisfy Christa, while reinforcing her parents' view of both of them— Good Daughter Christa overcoming all the odds and being a shining success; Bad Daughter Ruby never quite living up to her potential.

She blew out a breath. She hadn't fulfilled her potential because it hadn't been *her* dreams she'd been chasing in the first place. Would winning her parents' approval that way—in direct competition with Christa—have made her happy anyway? She suddenly doubted it. Surely you shouldn't have to *win* your parents' love. Shouldn't it just be given?

'I don't want to compete with Christa any more.' She blinked as the truth settled over her. 'I'm *not* going to compete any more.'

She had to start living her own life, pursuing her own dreams.

Something deep inside Luis's chest started to burn.

Ruby met his gaze. 'I'm only ever going to be a disappointment to them, regardless of what I do. But I don't have to be a disappointment to myself.'

'You're not a disappointment to me. I think you're amazing.'

Their gazes caught and clung, and for a moment he thought... But then she rolled her eyes. 'You're going to be mightily disappointed if I don't manage to alienate your parents.'

In that moment he saw what he was asking of her. *Verdammt.* He was demanding she reprise the role of failure here with his family now. The same role her family had thrust her into. He pressed a hand to his brow. Not only was that unfair, it was *cruel*. 'We have to call off this charade.'

'What?' She swung back. *'Why?'*

'Because I now know how part of this is going to play out. You're going to be offered that partnership, but now you're not going to want it.'

Her mouth opened and closed. She rolled her shoulders. 'That's not a given.'

'Isn't it? You've just said that you're going to live your own dreams from now on, not anyone else's. We both know that partnership was never your dream. I cannot ask you to continue helping me when what you wanted has changed.'

'You weren't to know I'd change my mind! That's not your responsibility. You've kept your side of the bargain. Let me keep mine.'

'Except you're my friend, and I refuse to take advantage of you.'

'And what if I tell you I *want* to keep our charade going?'

Why on earth would she want to do such a thing when he knew how hard she found it to maintain this act with his parents?

She shot to her feet. 'I need time away from the real world, Luis. I need to work out what it is I *do* want. Despite my old dream, I don't want to be a criminal lawyer. It sounded terribly noble when I was a teenager, but the reality is it's high pressure, high stakes and cut-throat. *Not* my jam.'

As she spoke, she paced, waving her arms above her head. Watching her made his skin tighten and the blood in his veins heat.

'There are other ways to fight injustice. I just need to settle on one. Being here for the holidays will give me the time I need to do that.' Turning to face him, she slammed her hands to her hips. 'If we stop the charade then I have to go home.'

Blödsinn!

Nonsense.

'You can stay here for as long as you want.'

Planting her feet, she shook her head. 'No, I can't.' Her eyes narrowed. 'And do you really want to stop now when you're so close to finding out the truth?'

He hesitated. He didn't want Ruby leaving before she was ready to.

'Don't you want to find out why your mother has been acting so oddly? Don't you want to find out what's wrong?'

Of course he did, but—

'We're this close.' She held her thumb and finger an inch apart. 'I can feel it, can't you? The kid issue has really stirred things up.'

It had.

'Your instincts are true. There's a deeper reason your mother has been putting so much pressure on you.'

Things inside him clenched. 'You think I should be worried?'

'I don't know. What I do know is that they love you, and yet they've been pushing you to do something you've not been ready for. I know I've only known them for a few days, but it seems awfully out of character.'

'Yes.'

'And you want to get to the bottom of it.'

He did.

'So let's just get on with it.'

If there was some greater problem with his parents or the company or something else that hadn't occurred to him, he needed to know what it was and fix it.

She bent down to stare into his eyes. 'In return for helping you, I get an amazing holiday in the Swiss Alps, which, I might tell you, is pretty amazing. And the time to sort my life out.' She straightened, folding her arms. 'And the time to bolster my personal resources so I don't let my parents and Christa erode my confidence again. These aren't small things to me.'

He could help her with all of that. 'Very well. For the moment, we'll stick with the plan.'

'Good.' She moved across to run a finger over the bust on the mantelpiece. 'It might sound odd, but I want to prove that I can do this.'

Rather than seeing all the ways the situation he'd thrust her into was wrong and reinforced the lessons her wrong-thinking parents had instilled in her, he started to see how keeping her side of their bargain might give her a sense of accomplishment. He suddenly smiled.

She glanced back at him, her brows going up. 'What?'

'You're here because you want to help right a wrong. You're already fighting injustice, Ruby.'

She blinked, her smile piercing his chest. He did what he could to get his rapid heartbeat under control. 'If we're doing this, we're going in hard. No more easing them into it.'

She nodded. 'Understood.'

'We're having a tree delivered this afternoon.'

The four of them were at breakfast, and Luis noticed the interest that brightened Ruby's eyes at the mention of the tree. 'You get a real one?'

'Absolutely,' Claudia said. 'Do you not in Australia?'

'We have an artificial one. I mean, it's not unheard of to get a real tree, but it's summer there, so a bit different from here.' She straightened in a way that informed him she was going into combat. 'Also, it's better for the environment to not be chopping down trees.'

Walter smiled. 'We source our tree from a nearby sustainable farm.'

She deflated. 'Oh, okay, that's all right, then.'

Maybe she'd become a crusader for the environment. The thought had him smiling.

'You will be here to help trim it, won't you?' Claudia said.

Ruby glanced at him and raised an eyebrow. Last night they'd agreed to go in hard. He mentally girded his loins. The more time they spent in his parents' company, the better they'd be able to appal them with this mismatch of a marriage. 'Absolutely.'

'Ruby.' Walter smiled at her. 'You showed some interest in the Pissarro in the blue drawing room. After breakfast, would you like a little tour of some of the museum pieces we have?'

'You have actual pieces a museum would want? *Wow!* Yes, please. Have you ever had them valued?'

She planned to absolutely horrify his father with her materialism? Excellent.

'In that case, Luis—' Claudia glanced across at him '—perhaps you'll help me bring the decorations down?'

Usually, it was he and his father who brought them down from a storage cupboard on the first floor. He saw then his parents' strategy. They meant to divide and conquer.

Game on.

Biting back a grim smile, he nodded. 'Of course.'

Luis set the first of the boxes on a table in the hall. 'Is everything okay, Mutti? You haven't said much to me about my unexpected marriage. It's not like you.'

She glanced across. 'I haven't wanted to say anything that would offend you.'

He met her gaze. 'I would not want that either.' His words were softly spoken but an unmistakable thread of steel ran beneath them.

Claudia nodded. 'You have to know that both your father and I were surprised at the suddenness of your marriage. It was a shock. Despite my recent urgings for you to consider settling down, you didn't seem the least interested. In fact, you seemed quite against it.'

He straightened. 'So why, I wonder, would you continue to push me into something I was averse to?'

Her back was presented to him as she marched back up the stairs. 'Clearly, though, it's not something you were averse to.'

He gritted his teeth and set off after her.

'After all, here you are, married.'

'Blissfully and happily, as you always predicted. Why are you not then crowing and reminding me that mothers know best?'

If possible, her back became even more ramrod straight. Silently she filled his arms with the next load of boxes.

'I thought you would take your time and get to know your prospective bride. I thought you would take the time to be sure of your feelings…be sure that you were compatible.'

'Like you and Vati?'

She spun to stare at him.

He lifted a shoulder. 'The two of you were sensible and yet it still didn't work out for you.'

Her swift intake of breath speared into the centre of him, but without another word, she grabbed a box and led the way back downstairs. 'Luis, I know that the divorce affected you badly.'

'Not as badly as it affected the two of you.'

She blinked.

'All I'm saying is that the two of you did it the sensible way, and yet it still ended in divorce. It didn't turn out the way either of you hoped. From what I can see, there is no right or wrong way to go about marriage.'

'But there is! Have you not heard the adage *marry in haste repent at leisure*? Luis, you've taken no time to ensure you and your new bride's values align. You have rushed into something that I greatly fear will lead to pain and heartache.'

'My heartache or yours, Mutti?'

She swung to him with an audible gasp.

'This is because yesterday Ruby said she wasn't interested in having children, isn't it?'

'But, Luis, surely you want children?'

'No.'

She stared at him before shaking her head. 'You will change your mind, and what then?'

'The thought of children has never filled me with enthusiasm.'

She slashed a hand through the air. 'Those are Ruby's words, not yours.'

'It's a sentiment I share.'

She gestured around. 'What about passing all of this down to the next generation? What about doing your duty? Who will take over the company if you do not have children?'

Things inside him went cold. Was that all he was to his parents—a succession plan? Had their love come with conditions after all?

Nausea churned in his stomach. 'If that was truly important to you, Mutti, then you should've had more children. Perhaps one of them would've been more *dutiful* than I.'

She drew herself up to her full height, her eyes flashing. 'Your father and I couldn't have more children after you were born.'

He blinked. He hadn't known that.

'I can't believe, after all we've given you, that you would be so selfish and so determined to break our hearts.'

His jaw dropped, but she fled up the stairs. A moment later he heard the door to her room slam. He brought the rest of the decorations down on his own.

CHAPTER SEVEN

THE TREE WAS GINORMOUS, its topmost branches reaching up to brush the railings of the first-floor landing, and Ruby clasped her hands beneath her chin and simply stared. She'd not seen it arrive so she had no idea how many men it had taken to wrestle it into place, but it stood there now, tall and proud, in this amazingly grand foyer as if it belonged there. The dark green branches against all of the dark wood and cast-iron work looked somehow timeless—as if this exact same tableau could have existed two hundred years ago in the exact same spot.

'What do you think?'

Walter smiled down at her, and all she could do was lift her shoulders in a helpless shrug. 'It's beautiful.'

She should've made some comment about it being as venerable as the family's art collection. Or their wine collection. Walter had given her a tour of that when he'd found out how much she'd enjoyed a holiday to Australia's Barossa Valley.

She had no recollection of how they'd even got onto the topic.

Walter was interested in everyone and everything. He was fascinating, warm and charming. His humour—gentle and kind—was a balm to the soul. Perhaps especially to one that felt as ragged as hers. Not that she could blame her raggedness entirely on the stress of maintaining her charade of grasping, greedy and totally unsuitable daughter-in-law. An awful lot of the blame for that rested with the recent discoveries she'd made about herself and her life and the direction she now wanted to take.

Not that she had an actual destination in mind. All she knew was she no longer wanted to be on the road she'd taken. She wanted to do something that made her soul glad, that made her feel as if she was doing something worthwhile.

She twisted her hands together. Was she really going to upend her life so completely?

Shaking her head, she pushed the thought away. There'd be time enough for that later. Instead, she risked another glance at Luis's father.

Walter had gone out of his way to entertain her today, to ensure she'd enjoyed his tour, wanting to engage her thoughts on every topic he'd touched upon. It had taken every ounce of her strength to not fall under his spell. It was awful maintaining their fraud in the face of such kindness.

But maintain it she would. For Luis's sake. *And*

for her own. She needed to know she could hold fast to a plan in the face of opposition. She needed to prove to herself that she had the strength to live the life she now wanted.

Luis and Claudia entered the grand foyer at precisely the same moment, but from opposite directions—Luis from the left and Claudia from the stairs. She took in their closed faces, the careful way they avoided each other's eyes, and frowned. Something had clearly happened while she and Walter had been undertaking their art and wine tour.

Which could be a good thing.

But a second glance at Luis's face had her dismissing that thought.

Walter glanced at her, a question in his eyes. All she could do was shrug. Turning back, he clapped his hands. 'Ruby claims she's never seen a bigger Christmas tree.'

She followed his lead because she'd do anything to rid Luis's face of that expression. 'The biggest in a private house,' she corrected. 'Though, as your house is more like a castle…'

All three of them started to shake their heads. She raised her hands. 'I know! I know! It's not fortified. Still…' Mischief shuffled through her. 'Have you never been tempted to put in a moat?'

All three swung to her as one, alarm racing across their faces. 'No!'

Chuckling, she pulled her phone from her pocket.

'I'll show you my family's Christmas tree and you'll see why I'm in such awe of this baby.'

Scrolling through the photos on her phone, she came to December the previous year and found one with her parents and Christa posing in front of their tree. 'Here we go.'

Luis and Claudia crowded beside her to get a better view. Across the way Walter smiled at her and winked. It warmed her to her very toes.

'This is your family?' Claudia asked, reaching for the phone, and then drawing back as if afraid of having her hand slapped away.

Ruby handed the phone across and then pointed. 'My mum and dad, and this is my cousin, Christa, who came to live with us when she was eleven.'

Claudia scrolled through all the photos of the previous Christmas, before returning to the first one. 'There are no photos of you.'

Her words pierced into the sorest part of Ruby's heart. Christa featured regularly in the family albums. Ruby not so much. Christa would gladly write Ruby out of the family history, but it hurt to think that her parents would go along with that.

Taking the phone and shoving it back into her pocket, she shrugged. 'I'm usually the photographer.'

Claudia opened her mouth, and Ruby sensed rather than saw Luis shake his head. Claudia closed her mouth again, and Ruby wished the floor would swallow her whole. How pathetic her life must seem to these people when not even her own family cared about having her in their record of family events.

'Come!' Claudia clapped her hands. 'Let's get a picture of you and Luis in front of the tree for you to send home to your family. We can have one prior to it being decorated and one after.' Claudia's eyes narrowed and she smiled...a little evilly if the truth be told. 'And then one with all of us with the tree, lights twinkling, as we toast with champagne. *Good* champagne.'

She imagined Christa's envy and her parents' shock. 'That sounds—' *Don't gush!* Though she had no hope of wiping the grin from her face. '—fabulous.'

'It's a brilliant idea!' Luis towed her over to the tree, pulled her phone from her pocket and thrust it at his mother. 'Smile your biggest smile at the camera, my little *Zaubermaus*.'

She couldn't help but laugh.

Claudia snapped a couple of shots and then said, 'Now look at each other.'

Ruby glanced up at Luis and the devilry dancing in his eyes had her grinning too, but slowly his grin faded, the devilry replaced with heat, and her smile faded too as her heart began to pound a hard tattoo in her chest. The dark green cotton of his long-sleeved tee stretched across his body, highlighting the broad lines of his shoulders and chest, arrowing down across a hard flat stomach. She remembered exploring those lines with her hands and lips, and her mouth dried as an ache started up deep inside—a pounding, pulsing surging of heat and lust. Her hand lifted to splay against his chest, Luis hissed in a breath—

'Ahem.'

Walter cleared his throat with a stridency that had her and Luis springing apart. *Dear God.* Cheeks burning, she took her phone, unable to look Claudia in the eye.

'Would you send me copies of those, my dear?'

'Sure.' It took a superhuman effort, but her voice sounded at least halfway normal. Sending the photos to the number Claudia recited gave her a chance to get her breath back and wrestle her wayward impulses back under some semblance of control.

When she finally turned, she found Walter and Luis unpacking the first of the boxes. An entire set of wooden nutcracker figurines emerged, painted in reds, greens and golds. 'Oh!' She touched one reverently. 'They're beautiful.'

'They've been handed down through the generations,' Claudia said from beside her. 'I treasure every single one of them.'

If they were hers, she would too. There were tiny tin bells in pretty pastel shades, coloured glass balls, Bohemian stars, Victorian era angels, tiny wooden sleighs and reindeer, not to mention more modern crystal pieces, all of them utterly exquisite. And, of course, there were Christmas lights. When the lights and ornaments were all in place, the four of them stood back to admire their handiwork.

Ruby couldn't feign anything in that moment. Wonder took up residence inside her, leaving room for nothing else. She couldn't remember the last time she'd truly experienced the magic of Christmas, but an effervescence of hope and awe filled her chest now, bringing a lump to her throat. Surely, just for a moment, it would be okay to let down her guard and treasure this.

Luis glanced at her and something in his eyes gentled. 'It's really something, isn't it?'

She nodded, not trusting herself to speak.

'We have something for you, Ruby.'

She started when Claudia spoke.

'As you just saw, everyone in the family has their own special ornament.'

Luis's was the most adorable gingerbread man.

'As this is your first Christmas as a member of our family, we have one for you too.'

She held out a box. Ruby stared at it until Luis nudged her. 'It won't bite, I promise.'

She couldn't make her smile work properly. 'Th…thank you.'

Nestled inside the box, in tissue paper, rested a crystal dove in flight. As she held it up by its satin ribbon, a thousand rainbows refracted from the etched wings. She couldn't utter a single syllable. Tears blurred her vision and a lump lodged in her throat.

Luis's arm went about her shoulder and wrapped her in warmth. 'I think, Mutti, we can safely say she loves it.'

And then both Claudia and Walter wrapped their arms around them too, and Ruby had no hope of keeping two of her tears from spilling onto her cheeks.

She dashed them away when they all parted again. 'Thank you. I've never had my very own Christmas ornament before. It's beautiful.'

Claudia beamed at her. 'Luis, set it next to your gingerbread man.'

When that was done, Walter held up the switch for the lights. 'Are we ready?'

Bouncing on the balls of her feet, she held her breath…

Voila! The tree lit up with what seemed like a hundred tiny lights, making her breath catch. She couldn't help clapping like a child. 'It's perfect!'

More photos were taken and a lovely bottle of champagne opened and they toasted the tree, and the season and each other, and just for a moment it felt perfect.

Imagine what it would be like to be a part of this every year.

She tried to halt the images that flooded through her. She couldn't fall for all of this magic. It wasn't hers to fall for. It would *never* be hers. Her eyes stung but she ignored them. She refused to let them turn towards Luis. He wasn't hers either.

Glancing around for distraction, she found Claudia staring into another box. Something about the disconsolate slope of the older woman's shoulders caught at her and had her moving across. 'Did we forget to put some of the ornaments up?'

'No, no. It's just… Well, would you like to see?'

Some sixth sense told her that she *didn't* want to see. Some sixth sense told her she'd just played into Claudia's hands, though she couldn't explain what exactly it was that made her feel manipulated. She couldn't very well back away now, though, so she shrugged. 'Sure.'

Across the way, she caught Luis's gaze and hoped he read her 'Help me!' signal.

Claudia pulled out two further ornaments— one a golden crystal candle and the other an exquisite snowflake. 'I've had these for a long time. They've always been meant for Luis's children.'

And just for a flash, she could imagine those children as vividly as Claudia must. She swallowed and nodded. 'They're very beautiful.'

'Yes. And it is my dearest wish…'

It took all of Ruby's strength to step away. 'I'm sorry to disappoint you, Claudia.' She counted to three, then five. 'I'm sure they won't go to waste, though. They'll make lovely gifts for friends.'

Luis moved across, his gaze whipping between

Ruby and his mother. 'I didn't mention it earlier, but Ruby and I have plans for this evening.' He took Ruby's arm. 'I hope you don't mind if we excuse ourselves.'

'Oh, but I thought,' Claudia started, but Walter's hand on her shoulder halted her. She forced a smile. 'Well, enjoy yourselves. I hope you have a nice time.'

'Before I forget,' Walter said, 'Hans called about the hockey. He was hoping you could play this week.'

The hockey...?

Ruby drew herself up to her full height and turned to Luis. 'Hockey?'

'I play in a team with some friends and—'

He'd not even finished before she was shaking her head. 'No.'

His frown almost looked real. 'Ruby, I've been a part of this team for years and—'

'That was when you were a single man. You're married now and you have responsibilities to me.'

'Ruby, sweetheart, be reasonable—'

She poked a finger in his chest. 'I know what happens when single men get together. You go out somewhere for a drink afterwards and there'll be women and—'

'I swear to you—'

She folded her arms and glared. *'No.'*

'Ruby,' Walter cut in with his trademark warmth, 'it is nothing more than a bit of harmless fun. Do you not think it important to maintain your own pursuits and interests, even though you're now married?'

'Harmless?' she screeched. 'Do you know how many marriages fail due to infidelity? Oh, it starts out harmless enough, but in the blink of an eye a man falls under the spell of a pretty smile and an ample bust…and his friends will egg him on. Oh, later he'll regret it bitterly, but the damage will be done. Or,' she added, when Walter opened his mouth to argue, 'the other partner, feeling neglected, seeks solace elsewhere.'

The shocked silence made her inwardly cringe, but she kept her spine straight. She'd wanted her words to sound threatening. And they did. In a weird way she was almost proud of that. 'Start as we mean to go on, I say.' She hiked up her chin. 'And, Luis, that means no hockey.'

'Let's talk about this later,' he said, looking marvellously shaken.

'Babe, there's nothing to talk about.'

Lifting her hand, he brought it to his lips. 'I'd never do anything you were so against, sweetheart.'

Claudia and Walter exchanged worried glances and satisfaction settled in the pit of her stomach. They were hiding something, and they were pushing Luis to fix it without sharing the problem with him. It wasn't fair, and she'd help him get to the bottom of it if it was the last thing she did.

'Come, I promised you a romantic dinner, just the two of us.'

She didn't point out that they were hardly dressed for such an occasion. Instead, with a smile and a wave in her in-laws' direction, she let Luis tow her away. But she didn't let herself relax until they'd driven out of the tall gates and away from the villa full of dreams that she couldn't make come true.

Luis glanced at the woman beside him, barely recognisable as the entitled spoiled woman he'd towed from the house minutes ago. 'You're brilliant at this.'

Her smile speared into his chest, reminding him of that fraught moment when they'd had their picture taken. She'd wanted him, she hadn't been able to hide it. And if his parents hadn't been there, he'd have had her—again and again if he'd had any say in it. On the floor. On the stairs. On the landing.

Damn it!

She'd told him that if they continued their affair, her emotions would become engaged. He couldn't do that to her. It'd make him all that was selfish and thoughtless. He clenched his teeth so hard his jaw started to ache. Thank God his parents *had* been there.

'You're right, though. Your father is an utter sweetheart, which doesn't make things easy.' She turned to face him more fully. He concentrated on staring at the road ahead. 'Lying to them is a challenge, but something is going on, Luis, and I want to help you work out what it is.'

He knew what was going on. His hands tightened about the steering wheel. His mother had a very set picture in her mind for how she wanted him to live his life, and, if he strayed from it, all he could expect from her were censure and condemnation. Walter would make not the smallest of protests. He'd always wanted Claudia to have whatever it was that she wanted, and he'd make sure she got it regardless of the expense—even if it cost his son's happiness.

This morning Walter had taken him aside and asked him to reconsider his decision about not having children. 'At least tell your mother you'll reconsider in a couple of years. Give her some hope.'

'You want me to lie?'

Walter had paled. 'You cannot know what the future will bring, Luis.'

Luis had simply walked away feeling more alone than he'd ever felt in his life.

Pushing those dark thoughts aside, he drove into the nearby town, and parked the car at the same moment fat flakes started to fall from the sky. They'd had plenty of snow so far this season, but it was the first time Ruby had seen it actually snow, and she watched it now with a wide-eyed wonder that pushed away some of the greyness that had settled over him.

Jumping out of the car and lifting a hand, she caught a snowflake on her palm and watched it melt. 'Oh!'

She turned to him with those wide eyes and he couldn't help huffing out a laugh. Tiny flakes dotted her hair, making her look like an angel. He might be feeling as if his world were coming apart, but having Ruby here with him helped. Grabbing her hand, he led her into a nearby tavern and planted her at a table in the window. Returning from the bar, he set a mug of glühwein in front of her.

She brought the steaming mug to her nose and inhaled the scent before sipping it, her eyelids fluttering in appreciation. 'This smell and taste will now remind me of Christmas for ever.' Her gaze caught his. 'Thank you for this adventure, Luis. I don't think I've said that enough. All of this, it's once-in-a-lifetime stuff.'

Reaching across the table, he took her hand. 'I know I'm preoccupied with other things, but having you here helping me means a lot, Ruby.'

Her gaze lowered back to her glühwein and after a quick squeeze, she reclaimed her hand. It left him feeling curiously adrift, but she was right. Touching was a bad idea. *So stop doing it.*

While it might feel good to have Ruby on his

side, he couldn't get used to it. More to the point, he couldn't let *her* get used to it.

'What happened with your mother?'

It had been that obvious, huh? 'Tell me what happened with my father first.'

'Nothing of any note. I mean, he's the loveliest man, but that's not news. I remained strong, though, and was hideously mercenary, wanting to know the price of absolutely everything.' She traced a finger around her coaster. 'I lost it a bit, though, when we were decorating the tree. That was…' she wrinkled her nose and he tried to not notice how adorable it was '…kind of special. And then the dove… It all took me off guard.'

She deserved that kind of warmth every year. How could her family not see what a treasure this woman was?

'But I think I managed to claw things back with the hockey thing.'

Her satisfaction had him laughing. 'You did indeed. I'm not sure what appalled my parents more—your demands or my easy capitulation.'

'We are the dream team!' They high-fived. 'Okay, you and your mum?'

That dark cloud descended again. 'She accused me of being selfish and not doing my duty.'

'Because…?'

'Who will carry on the family name, who will inherit the villa, who will run the company after me if I don't have children?'

Her brow wrinkled. 'I don't get it. If having grandchildren was so important to her, you'd have known about it all your life. It wouldn't be a recent thing. It would've been part of the family narrative—a thing they were looking forward to you doing...like graduating college.' She bit her lip. 'Why has it become important *now*?'

He frowned then too. It *had* only become important these last few months.

Hazel eyes raked his face. 'And as all of this is a bolt out of the blue, you now feel you hardly know her.'

He pulled back, tried to not look so confused, so...*hurt*. Ruby saw too much. 'I believed my parents when they told me they wanted me to follow my own dreams. Now it feels like a lie. It feels as if they've manipulated me without me being aware of it, saying what they know I want to hear.' His hands clenched. 'Now it feels as if their love is conditional when all of this time, I believed otherwise.'

Ruby was shaking her head before he could finish. 'They love you every bit as much as you love them.'

He hated himself for how much he wanted to believe her. He didn't *want* to believe he was just a means to an end to them.

'Something's happened. Recently. We just have to figure out what.'

Not at the moment. He was tired of it. 'Are you hungry?'

She blinked. 'It's a bit early for dinner.'

'Want to amble around the Christmas markets first, then?'

'Christmas markets?' Her eyes lit up.

And just like that the weight on his shoulders lifted. He gestured out of the window. 'You can just see the town square from here, which is where they set up.'

'I've been trying not to stare out of the window.'

'Why not?'

'Because it's like every dream of a white Christmas I've ever had, except better. Snow, fir trees, Swiss chalets, mountains! I swear there's a Christmas wreath on every door. The only thing missing is a robin redbreast.' She turned those extraordinary eyes to him. 'Do you have robins in Switzerland?'

'You're more likely to see one in spring.' He spread his hands. 'If you're enjoying it so much, why are you not glorying in it?' It was the reason he'd chosen this table, after all.

'Because we were having a serious conversation. It's important to work out what's happening with your parents.'

'We've done enough for one day.' He nodded at her drink. 'Drink up, swee— Ahem… Ruby.' *Just Ruby.* 'It's Christmas. We're entitled to a little fun.'

With an excited squirm that burrowed into his chest, she finished her glühwein before winding her scarf around her neck and pulling on her coat. 'Maybe I'll find gifts to send home for Christmas. Something particularly Swiss would be—' her eyes danced '—perfect.'

He stabbed a finger to the table. 'We're going to find something perfect for Horrid Cousin Christa. Something that will have her gnashing her teeth in envy.'

She gurgled back a laugh. 'If I were a better person, I'd be above such things.'

'Blödsinn.' He tucked her hand in the crook of his elbow. 'If she were a better person, she'd be happy for you and all of your successes.'

The Christmas markets were crowded and the air buzzed with good cheer and smelled of cinnamon, cookies and a hint of rum. Ruby wanted to look at everything and experience every single moment to its fullest. Her delight reminded him of when he was a child and the season had held such wonder for him.

When had he lost that? Had he become so focussed on work and success and grooming himself to take over from his father that he'd lost sight of everything else the world had to offer?

'You're looking serious.'

He crashed back. 'I...' Swallowing, he gestured around. 'This, it is fun.'

'And...?'

'I just wondered... When did I stop having fun?'

Her brows shot up. 'You've been fun for as long as I've known you. You were great fun in Vegas. And we've had fun since arriving in Switzerland.'

All true. Maybe it was Ruby who made the difference?

He shied away from the thought. Even if she did, he and long-term commitment did *not* go hand in hand.

'Clearly you do things you enjoy—like skiing and playing hockey.'

So why did he now feel as if he'd fallen into a rut without even knowing it?

She planted her hands on her hips and stared at him, lips pursed. He rolled his shoulders. 'What?'

'Could this be what your mother's machinations are all about?'

'What?'

'You feeling so...jaded.'

'I'm not—'

He couldn't finish the sentence. *Jaded.* The word lodged inside him like a burr he couldn't shake off. 'I can't be jaded,' he growled.

'Why not?'

'I have *everything*. I'm healthy, young, successful. I have family and friends who care about me.'

'The family is acting weird at the moment, though,' she pointed out.

True, but... His hands clenched. 'I lead an extraordinarily privileged life. I have no right to feel *jaded*.'

'That's not the way the world works, and you know it.' She turned to a nearby vendor and pointed at the *pain d'espices*, held up two fingers, before pulling some coins from her pockets and paying for them. She handed one of the slices to Luis before biting into her own.

Her eyes closed in bliss as the spiced honey bread hit her tongue and Luis had to drag his gaze away from that lovely mouth and slam a lid on all thoughts of kissing her.

'Mothers are supposed to have a kind of sixth sense where their children are concerned.'

Hers didn't. 'Why whip me with words like responsibility and duty, then? Surely that's counter-intuitive?'

'Maybe she's hoping to shock you into finding what will give your life the extra meaning it's missing. Maybe she thinks being married and having children will do that.'

'I—' He didn't know what to say.

She patted his arm. 'I didn't say it had to make sense.'

He bit into his honey cake, chewed and swallowed. 'If your hypothesis is correct, then what we need to do is convince her that my life is filled with joy.' That he needed neither wife nor children to make him happy.

She stared at him with an unreadable expression.

It took a superhuman effort not to fidget. 'What?'

'Wouldn't it be easier to simply work out what gave you joy and do that instead? Rather than pretending? If she sees you truly happy—'

'There's nothing wrong with my life, Ruby.'

There wasn't.

She was silent for a long moment. 'Do you know, I haven't asked my question yet.'

What was she talking about?

'You know—you got to ask a personal question on the proviso that I could ask one in return.'

He clapped a hand to his brow. 'I forgot! What is your question?'

'I don't know yet.'

He couldn't say why, but he didn't believe her.

'But when I do, I'll ask it. Ooh, look!' She pointed behind him. 'That's my parents sorted.'

He followed her finger and started to laugh. 'A cuckoo clock?'

'It's perfection.'

She also bought them a set of nutcracker ornaments. For Christa she chose a beautiful handmade woollen scarf and matching hat. At the last moment she seized a box of speciality chocolates and added them to her growing pile of purchases. 'That's my contribution to their Christmas dinner this year.' There was nothing mean-spirited about any of it.

When her shopping was done, he bundled her into a nearby chalet and bought them plates of raclette—melted cheese with boiled potatoes, thin slices of ham, and pickled onions—which they devoured seated at a long table with other diners. It was rowdy and fun, but all the while the word *jaded* went round and round in his mind.

Could it be that his mother did sense that thread of dissatisfaction running through him? Did she believe a wife and children would solve it? 'We're going to change tack a bit. I'm going to rediscover my inner joy.'

She glanced up, immediately alert. 'Okay, how?'

'By doing what we did in Vegas—by having fun.' Mischief shifted through him. 'Do you like sledding?'

Her eyes widened. 'Really?' she breathed.

He nodded.

'Also, this may not be considered *sexy*, but I have a secret addiction to Scrabble.'

'Words *are* sexy, Luis. I'm a lawyer. I *work* with words.' She slapped a hand to her chest. 'And I'm a very good Scrabble player.'

He'd look forward to their first game.

She toyed with the food on her plate. 'I think being married and having you gave your parents a lot of joy. I think that's why they want it for you too.'

He blinked.

'I think there's still a lot of feeling between them.' She met his gaze. 'Why did they divorce?'

He tried to shrug off a sudden heaviness.

'They've never discussed the reasons with me. The most I've been able to get from them is that they wanted different things from marriage.'

'And yet they've never remarried. And they couldn't bear to lose each other so they've done all they can to remain close. I think they still love each other, Luis…as more than friends,' she added when he opened his mouth. 'And I think *that's* what's at the heart of this mystery, I just don't know how.'

He tried to get his head around what she was suggesting. Ice tripped down his spine. The divorce had been traumatic. He never wanted to see either of his parents in such emotional turmoil again.

Her touch on his arm dragged him back. 'I could be wrong. But watch and see how well they take care of each other, and how aware they are of each other.'

Slowly, he nodded. Could his mother's desire for him to settle down somehow be rooted in her own unconscious desire for a reunion with his father? And if it was, how could he help reconcile her to the fact that friendship would serve her much better than love ever would?

CHAPTER EIGHT

RUBY AND LUIS spent the next few days sledding down the slope behind the villa, building a snowman, playing rowdy games of Scrabble in the evenings and quietly finding new ways for Ruby to be slyly obnoxious.

The sledding was glorious. Except…well… Sharing a sled with Luis, his arms wrapped securely around her as he taught her how to steer, was *too* glorious. It made her heart pound and her pulse flutter, and if the excitement and heat it generated could've found an outlet during the nights when they were alone in their beautiful suite it would've been perfect.

But it didn't.

So it wasn't.

She had to keep reminding herself that none of this was real. Falling in love with Luis would be destructive. In the same way competing with Christa had been. It wouldn't set her life on the right path, wouldn't make her happy. She'd simply be repeating bad patterns and she was done with all of that. From now on she was only chasing those things that enhanced her life, that added to her happiness, and made her feel good about herself. Falling in love with Luis would have the opposite effect. To feel anything deeper than friendship for him would be foolhardy. She *would* keep her head.

And her heart.

And yet the heat between them continued to build. She knew he felt it too. She sensed it in the reluctant way his hands released her whenever he helped her to her feet, in the dark hunger that flashed through his eyes at different moments, in the way his nostrils flared whenever she was near. He never acted on it though, and she told herself she was glad of it.

She did what she could to focus on what they *did* do instead. They had races down the slope, which she hardly ever won, but the wind in her face and sheer rush made her feel alive. The setting, too, stole her breath. The glittering snow and the dark green of the alpine spruces all around, not to mention the towering mountains, made her feel as if she'd stepped into the pages of *Heidi*, one of her favourite childhood books. And running back to the top of the hill at least helped rid her of some of that banked-up energy.

Building the snowman filled her with a ridiculous amount of glee. It was as much fun as building a sandcastle at the beach, only better because

Christa wasn't there to start building a neighbouring eight-storey sand skyscraper.

For the first two nights, Claudia and Walter played Scrabble too, but after that they left her and Luis to it, claiming they couldn't keep up. Scrabble was the one game at which she could always beat Christa, which meant her family never played it. Luis provided her with stiff competition and she gloried in the challenge of it.

And now that she'd finally got into the swing of things, her assumed obnoxiousness became a secret source of hilarity.

When Luis's parents asked if they'd like a party to celebrate their marriage, she'd said, 'Absolutely not,' with as much spoiled-princess entitlement as she could muster. 'Do you want to wreck this marriage? For heaven's sake, we've not been married a month. We don't need the pressure of people asking us questions we don't yet know the answers to.'

'What kind of questions?'

The concern in Walter's voice had twisted her heart. 'Like where we're going to live.'

Claudia had blinked at that. 'I thought you were going to live here.'

'This will be our Swiss base, of course, but we'll need an Australian base as well. And somewhere more central on the continent, like London or Rome.'

'Heavens,' Claudia had murmured.

Ruby had heaved another sigh. 'Then there'd be the questions about what we plan to do in terms of work.'

Walter had stiffened. 'I see.'

She'd smiled at him sweetly. 'Good.'

'You're right.' Claudia hadn't been able to keep the edge from her voice. 'A party is probably not a good idea.'

Another time Ruby had flounced into the blue drawing room, which they now used because she'd insisted it was the nicest room in the whole *castle*, with a pile of magazines clutched to her chest. 'Honey bun…' She'd curled into Luis's side. 'Wouldn't it be nice to have, not just a sitting room and bedroom, but our own little self-contained part of this castle—you know, with a kitchen and dining room—so we could entertain, but also feel as if we're living on our own? And maybe even a second bedroom for when you snore.'

His eyes had twinkled. 'Whatever you want, my little *Zaubermaus.*'

'And we could decorate! Look!' She'd shown them all pictures of ridiculously tacky designs that she'd gushed over. Claudia had excused herself claiming a headache. Walter had silently poured himself a Scotch.

One night she'd made a scene about Luis not wanting to be seen with her in public, had accused him of being ashamed of her. She'd told him that if he wanted to prove he loved her, he had to take her to see the ballet at the Zurich Opera House and to dinner at a new, ridiculously overpriced restaurant. When he'd capitulated, she'd then claimed she had nothing to wear so what was the point of it all anyway?

She'd stormed out to lock herself in their suite, hoping her bad behaviour would breach his parents' walls and give him a chance to ferret out what was going on.

No such luck, but the next day he'd surprised her with tickets to the ballet, a reservation at said restaurant, and later that morning a designer dress had arrived for her. The look Claudia and Walter had exchanged made it worth it.

The price for that particular stunt, though, had been high. She and Luis had then had to spend a night dolled up to the nines—and he looked ridiculously delectable in a tuxedo and snowy white dress shirt—doing their best not to feast their eyes on one another. The food had been delectable, the ballet extraordinary, but she hadn't been able to focus on any of it, too aware of the man beside her.

The trip home had been fraught, and small talk too difficult. When they'd arrived back at the villa, he'd made some abrupt excuse about needing to check something in his study. She'd fled to their suite and locked herself in their bedroom to prevent herself from doing something she knew she'd regret. She had enough toxic relationships in her life. She wasn't adding another to the list. Falling in love with Luis was out of the question. To do something so stupid would only prove her family right. Her hands had clenched so hard she'd started to shake. She was tired of feeling like a loser. It was time to be a winner.

On Christmas Eve, they found themselves alone in the villa, both Claudia and Walter having gone into the office—probably to get away from her. Ruby flopped down on the sofa in front of the gently crackling fire in the blue drawing room. 'Are we any closer to finding out what's going on?'

He fell down into the sofa opposite, rubbing both hands back through his hair until it stuck up every which way and she had to fight the urge to smooth it down again.

When he didn't answer, she said, 'Do you think they're in love with each other?'

He shrugged. 'They've always been that way with one another.'

She folded her arms, irritation inexplicably itching through her. 'Sorry, it was a stupid question. If you don't believe in love, how could you possibly tell if someone else was in love?'

He glanced across. 'I can recognise when someone is infatuated.'

'People don't stay infatuated for thirty years, Luis.'

'People delude themselves in any number of ways. You're a lawyer, you must've seen that.'

She snorted. 'In boring business law?'

He leaned forward. 'Speaking of work and jobs—'

'No.' She didn't want to talk about that. She still had no idea what her future looked like. She needed to prove herself here first, help Luis get to the bottom of this parental mystery, before she could focus on herself and her future. It didn't make sense, but once she'd achieved that it felt as if her future would become clear to her. 'I want to ask my personal question—the one you owe me.'

He eased back, his face guarded. 'Why do I feel as if this is something I'm not going to want to answer?'

'I didn't want to hear that I'd been wasting my time trying to compete with Christa—using her measure of success as my measure of success— but I'm glad I've faced that particular truth all the same.'

He frowned. 'You think there's something I need to face?'

'No.' She huffed out a breath. 'You seem to have your head screwed on a whole lot better than me.'

His face softened. 'Sweet Ruby, there are rea-sons—' He suddenly choked. 'Sorry, *Ruby*. Just Ruby. My circumstances have been vastly differ-ent from yours and...'

He trailed off, and she dismissed it with a wave of her hand, hoping it hid the way his endearment affected her. She loved it when he called her sweet Ruby. *Adored it.*

She swallowed. That couldn't be good. She needed to keep her emotional walls strong and unbreachable if she didn't want to leave with a broken heart. Where Luis was concerned, she had a major weakness. Giving into it, though, would be emotional suicide.

Girding her loins, she met his gaze. 'I don't want to challenge you about the way you're living your life. I just want to know why you don't believe in love.'

Those blue eyes darkened and for a moment she swore she saw pain there, but then he blinked and it was gone. 'I know it's a terribly personal question, and if you don't want to answer I'll understand.'

'But we have a deal.'

She sent him a weak smile. 'I'd let you off.'

He shook his head. 'You and I have come a long way, Ruby. I owe you.'

'No, you don't!'

'And you deserve the truth. As you foretold at the beginning of this journey, you've become a dear friend.'

Her eyes burned. She blinked. *Hard.*

'We won't lose sight of each other once this adventure is over.'

'No,' she croaked over the lump in her throat.

'The truth is, I stopped believing in romantic love when my parents divorced.'

But...he'd only been fourteen.

'I realised then—and this is a belief that has only grown—that if two good people who believe themselves totally in love and marry, and yet their marriage still fails despite their best efforts, then...' He trailed off with a shrug.

She frowned. 'Then what?'

'Then this notion of love is a lie. I know my parents cared about each other. I know they wanted the best for each other. If two people like that can't make a marriage work, then something is fundamentally wrong.'

'Like love being a lie,' she murmured.

'Exactly! I saw the devastation caused by believing that lie. They felt as if they'd let each other down, had betrayed each other.' His nostrils flared. 'They felt like failures.'

She leaned towards him. 'The notion that love can conquer all is the lie, Luis, not love itself. Sometimes love simply isn't enough.'

'The reason love isn't enough is because it's a myth.'

'Then what about all of those marriages that last happily for a lifetime? Don't they prove that love exists?'

'I think it is simply a case that those people have grown together in the same ways, in the same direction. The delusion is never tested, and therefore never fractures for them.' One shoulder lifted. 'They are lucky. But it is an odds game— and the statistics show us that forty per cent of marriages in Switzerland end in divorce, fifty per cent in the States… I must look up the Australian statistics.'

'It's been dropping,' she said mechanically, her mind a whirl. 'I think it's currently at thirty-three per cent, but fewer people are getting married so…'

'So…' he agreed.

She shook herself. 'You mention statistics. According to them sixty per cent of marriages in Switzerland are successful. The odds would be in your favour.'

His eyes flashed. 'I'm not risking the kind of trauma my parents experienced *on a bet*. And tell me, how would I satisfy a wife who did believe in romantic love? Such a woman would always want more than I could ever give. Why risk it?'

'Romantic love *does* exist, Luis. And it can be wonderful.' To cut himself off from all of that…

He shrugged. 'Most people would agree with you.'

She shivered. He looked so resolute. And alone.

'It is why we need to be careful with one another, Ruby.'

Her head snapped back. 'If I were to fall in love with you, Luis, I'd be the one to suffer, not you.'

'And the fact I would loathe and hate myself for what I'd done to you means nothing?'

Her jaw dropped. Hauling it back into place, she rubbed a hand across her chest. He was right. They needed to be *very* careful. 'You won't fall in love with me, and I won't fall in love with you.'

He nodded. 'That is our agreement.'

She nodded too, but the ice trickling through her veins refused to warm. She couldn't fall in love with this man. He would shatter her heart into a million little pieces. She was finally finding the courage to live life on her own terms. She needed to focus on the future, not pin her hopes on some guy who didn't believe in love.

Friends, that was all she and Luis would ever be. All she had to do now was ignore the insistent way her body ached for him.

She rolled her eyes. Piece of cake.

Christmas morning dawned and as soon as he woke, Luis glanced across to the windows. Fat white flakes fell from the sky and he grinned. Ruby would be over the moon. To her, a white Christmas was magical, and seeing it through her eyes made it feel magical to him too.

It was still early, but...

Throwing the covers back, he tiptoed across to the bedroom door and pressed an ear to it. Was she awake yet? Was that movement he—?

Without warning, the door opened and he

stumbled forward. Arms slid around him in an effort to right him—Ruby's arms—but she staggered at his unexpected weight. Before they could crash to the carpet, he slipped an arm about her waist and righted them both.

'What on earth…?' she squeaked, staring up at him, hands planted against his chest. Her pupils dilated and her breath sawed in and out. 'I…'

Her words faltered at whatever she saw in his face. She moistened her lips and he nearly groaned out loud. One Christmas kiss…what would it hurt?

'Merry Christmas, Ruby.'

'Merry Christmas, Luis.'

The husky words brushed across his skin. Just one kiss…

Lowering his mouth to hers, he claimed her lips in what he told himself would be a friendly, casual kiss—one that displayed nothing more than the cheer of the day. How he could lie to himself so spectacularly, he had no idea. The moment their lips touched, hunger torched through him and before he knew it he'd gathered her close, his mouth devouring hers.

She gasped, and the parting of her lips allowed his tongue to slide across hers and he had no idea if she'd meant to push him away or not, but then her tongue was dancing with his and her arms were around his neck, pulling him closer and his mind blanked and he fell into a world of warmth and delight. Need sparked, flared and raged out of control. He had her backed up and them both falling across the bed before he knew what he was about.

Stunned eyes stared up into his. The body beneath him arched against him, seeking release for the hunger they'd incinerated. He wanted to respond, his fingers ached to pull up the hem of her nightgown, shape her breasts in his hands and trail kisses down her stomach to the juncture of her thighs, where he'd apply himself to her pleasure with a diligence that would have her writhing and his name a chant on her lips.

He wanted that with a fierceness that shocked him. And yet...

If they made love, it might mean more to her than it would ever mean to him and—

He would not hurt her!

Rolling away with a groan, he stared up at the canopy of the bed and tried to get the pounding of his heart and wild longings under control.

'Ruby, I'm sorry, I—'

But she was already off the bed and the only answer was the soft click of the bathroom door closing.

He grabbed clothes from the dressing room and retreated to the sitting room, closing the bedroom door behind him. He dressed, folded his blankets. And then he sat on the sofa and waited.

It took a good forty minutes before that rotten

bedroom door opened. He shot to his feet. Staring at him, she hitched up her chin and opened her mouth, but he jumped in first. 'I'm sorry, Ruby. I said we needed to be careful with one another and then I go and lose my head like that. I didn't mean to. It wasn't planned.'

She stared at her hands. 'That's not much comfort, though, is it?'

'I promise to be more careful in future. I only put my ear to the door to see if you were awake, to wish you merry Christmas. I was excited because...'

Her gaze lifted to his.

Rolling his shoulders, he gestured to the window. 'It was snowing and it's your first white Christmas and...'

He felt like an idiot. Rubbing a hand across his nape, he couldn't meet her eyes. He was aware of her every rustle as she moved across to stare outside.

'Beautiful,' she murmured. 'Luis?'

She swung around and he forced his gaze to hers.

'I think it'd be for the best if we forget what just happened.'

He didn't deserve such grace. He—

'You said you'd be more careful in the future.'

He nodded.

'There's not much else to be asked for, then, is there? We both need to be more on our guard.'

'I—'

'And, Luis, it's Christmas. Let's enjoy it.'

He swore in that moment to make sure she enjoyed every moment of the day.

Breakfast was a merry affair with both of his parents in determinedly good spirits. After breakfast, gifts were exchanged. Ruby, he knew, had ordered gifts online and had them express-posted from Australia. She presented his father with a bottle of Australian wine that had the older man's eyes widening in appreciation. His mother received an exquisite Australian merino wool scarf and a set of Australian-designed Christmas baubles. Claudia immediately placed the scarf around her neck and hung the baubles on the tree.

To him, with a cheeky twinkle in her eyes, she gave a beautifully handcrafted roulette wheel and a blackjack set that made him grin as he recalled the fun they'd had in Vegas. His hands moved across the polished wood of the roulette wheel in appreciation. 'Perfection.'

Reaching under the tree, he pulled forth a small brightly wrapped box and pressed it into her hands. She frowned, suspicion rife in her eyes. 'We agreed to only give each other small gifts.'

'It *is* small, look at it! Far smaller than mine.' He made his eyes innocently wide. 'Open it, Ruby, stop stalling.'

With a grin, she did. He could see the way the pulse in her throat fluttered and had to shake away the vision of pressing his lips there. He'd like to—

Her gasp hauled him back into the moment.

Both of his parents murmured in appreciation as she lifted the teardrop ruby from its velvet box. It sparkled as it caught the light. 'Oh, Luis…' she whispered.

'Do you like it?'

Shaking herself, as if remembering the role she was supposed to be playing, she said, 'I love it. It's the most beautiful pendant I've ever seen.'

Reaching across, she kissed his cheek, and it took all his strength not to pull her into his lap and ravish her.

'Help me put it on.'

Turning, she lifted her hair away from her nape. He would *not* think about touching his lips there either. Fumbling with the catch, he finally secured it.

Swinging back, she said, 'What do you think?'

'Beautiful,' he croaked, staring at the delectable line of her throat and the pendant resting just above the shadow of her breasts.

Her eyes narrowed as if she knew the effect she was having on him. As if to punish him, she wrapped her arms around his neck and whispered in his ear, 'You will be getting this back too.'

He huffed out a laugh as she eased away. Another argument he'd look forward to. He'd bought this gift because it had made him think of her, and for no other reason than because he'd thought she'd like it. He would not be accepting it back.

'And, Ruby, there's a final gift from us,' Claudia said.

Claudia and Walter pushed a brightly wrapped present towards her, and her eyes widened. 'For me?'

'Well, it's for all of us really, but it's mostly for you, so we'd like you to open it.'

Oh, Lord! What had they gone and done? He shoved his hands into his back pockets. What fresh hell would he and Ruby have to negotiate now?

'Did you know about this?' she murmured.

He shook his head. It wasn't fair of him, he knew, but he'd hoped that today could be a cease-fire. He'd hoped they'd be able to relax their guard. He could see now how unrealistic that was.

Kneeling down beside it, Ruby tried to carefully unstick the tape from the gorgeous gold paper but Claudia, practically dancing in her chair, said, 'Go on, rip it!'

With a laugh, Ruby did as she was bid and then froze when she saw what the paper hid. She'd gone so still he crouched down beside her to see too, and offer whatever support she might need. Four individual boxes had been wrapped together and it wasn't until she pulled one of the boxes into her arms that he finally saw what she'd un-wrapped.

She hugged her box to her chest. 'Roller skates,' she whispered.

Claudia held her breath. 'Do you like them?'

Ruby's breath hitched, but she nodded.

He reached in and lifted a box that bore his name. 'You've bought us *all* roller skates?'

'Of course! Ruby said roller skating was her very favourite thing and I thought it was something we could all do together. In the ballroom. There's so much room in there. I mean, it's not as big as a rink, but we've had all the furniture removed in readiness.'

Ruby stared at them. 'You…?' Resting her forehead on the box, she burst into tears.

Claudia's and Walter's faces fell. Luis had no idea what to do. Eventually he sat on the floor, pulled Ruby onto his lap and rocked her. 'Hey, hey, my little *Zaubermaus*. Why are you crying? No one meant to upset you.'

Shaking her head, she lifted a hand as if wanting it to speak for her, but the sobs kept coming and she just wrapped the hand back around the box and let him rock her for the full five minutes it took for her to get her tears under control.

'I'm sorry,' she finally murmured, lifting her head and taking the handkerchief Luis pushed into her hands. She dried her eyes and blew her nose.

He tried not to relish the way she relaxed against him, as if she could think of no better place to be.

'I'm so embarrassed.'

'Don't be embarrassed, Ruby.' Claudia reached down to pat her arm. 'We're family now. We didn't mean to upset you or—'

'No, this is the best present ever!' She still hugged the box to her. 'I love the roller skates, it's just…' She struggled to her feet. 'Oh, Luis, let's sit like adults. Maybe then I'll stop feeling like such a child.'

They sat on the sofa again. She tucked her hair behind her ears and shrugged. 'When I was twelve, my very favourite thing was to roller skate. I just… I loved it the way a lot of girls my age seemed to love horses.'

He wished he still had her on his lap. 'What happened?'

She wrinkled her nose and he knew the answer before she could say it. 'Christa,' he growled.

Walter frowned. 'Your cousin who came to live with you?'

She gave a weak smile. 'It was about the only thing I was ever better at than she was.'

His mother drew herself up as if realising she wouldn't like this story. 'Go on, Ruby.'

'Well, Christa threw a temper tantrum about having to go roller skating—the whole tantrum-and-tears thing that worked on my parents like a charm. She said it upset her too much, that it reminded her of her parents who had died.'

'And your parents would no longer take you to the roller-skating rink?' Walter said gently.

'It wasn't just that. I'd have been more than happy to skate on my own.' She pushed her hair off her face and squared her shoulders. 'But my mother took my roller skates away and donated them to charity, told me we all had to make sacrifices for Christa. She'd lived with us for two years by that time and it felt like all I'd been doing was making sacrifices for her. It was the moment I realised Christa mattered more to them than I did.'

Luis's heart beat hard. *Verdammt.* What did he have to complain about? He had, until recently, experienced nothing but love and support from his parents.

She stared at the box in her lap. 'I haven't skated since that day, when I was twelve.'

Claudia shot to her feet. 'Would you like to skate now?'

Ruby hesitated, then, pushing her shoulders back, stood too. 'Yes, please!'

CHAPTER NINE

THE BALLROOM WAS a marvellously long room with a series of windows that marched down one wall overlooking what would usually be a manicured lawn, but was currently glittering virgin snow. A row of dark green conifers marked the boundary beyond, and, with their branches sprinkled with snow, they looked like frosty Christmas trees.

Donning knee and elbow pads, they made their first forays on their roller skates, wobbling, arm-windmilling, and hooting with laughter. The skating was every bit as much fun as Ruby remembered, and before long they were all gliding around the room with outsized grins on their faces.

This was what Christmas was supposed to be like.

This was how families were supposed to behave.

This was *perfect*.

Staring across at Claudia and Walter, she wished she could be the woman they wanted her to be. She wished this family were hers. She wished—

If wishes were fishes. She ought simply to be grateful she'd had the chance to experience a Christmas like this at all.

Walter and Claudia eventually retired to the sofas set up at one end of the ballroom, while she and Luis continued to skate. He was a natural, claiming it was due to the amount of time he'd spent playing ice hockey. Taking her hands, he skated her backwards, before grabbing her in a spin and then waltzing her around the room until she was breathless.

It was exhilarating.

It made her pulse sing.

And some inner voice prompted her to exalt in it. The fact Luis's parents remained in the room meant things couldn't get out of hand. It kept them *careful*.

And they *needed* to be careful. The kiss they'd shared this morning had rocked her to her very foundations, exploding as it had out of nowhere— a spark becoming an inferno with no warning. Thinking about it now made her pulse race. Deep inside hunger gnawed at her, but she did her best to ignore it.

Eventually George appeared in the doorway to announce that lunch was ready.

George, Ursula, and their two children Veronika and Mathias—home from university for the holiday—joined them, and the meal was rowdy and fun and not at all what Ruby had expected.

The affection in the air was easy and without awkwardness. A turkey, roasted to perfection, with all the trimmings was followed by an amazing plum pudding.

Too full of good food to do much of anything, they spent the afternoon resting. Luis explained that dinner would be leftovers and that they were just to help themselves whenever they became hungry.

'I'm never going to be hungry again,' she groaned in reply, making him laugh.

'Wait until after another session of roller skating. You will again build up an appetite, sweet Ruby.'

They were alone in the blue drawing room, stretched out on separate sofas in front of the fire, and she didn't have the energy to remonstrate with him. Turning to face him, she said, 'It was an inspired gift.'

He nodded.

'They continue in their efforts to connect with me.' She bit back a sigh. 'I thought I'd find this month difficult because acting's not my jam, not because your parents were determined to see the best of me.'

He folded his arms behind his head. 'The mixed messages we've been giving have complicated things. I should've thought that through more.'

She sat up. 'What are you talking about? What

mixed messages? I've been universally awful...
mostly. I mean, I couldn't be awful today because
it was Christmas—'

'Nobody is universally awful, Ruby.' He lifted
his head and sent her a slow grin that set her heart
thumping. 'They've had glimpses of the real you.
And hints enough about your family that they'd
be able to explain, if not excuse, your behaviour.
I can practically hear them telling themselves that
the lack of emotional security has manifested into
a need for material security.'

She rolled her eyes, but a lump lodged in her
chest.

'And while they're appalled at how I allow you
to browbeat me, they can't deny you also make
me happy.'

She made him happy? Something inside her
wanted to soar free, wanted to dance and skate
and sing. She held onto it for grim life, afraid to
set it free. 'I make you happy?'

'The sledding, the Scrabble games, the silly in
jokes...the feeling I have an ally. It has all been
wonderful, Ruby.'

She couldn't utter a single word.

'And nobody can help but notice the heat between us.'

Oh, God.

Lying back down, she stared resolutely at the
ceiling.

'I'm sorry. I didn't mean to make you uncomfortable.'

'I'm not uncomfortable.'

Liar, liar, pants on fire.

His words, though, sent hunger roaring through her—a hunger that craved satisfaction, relief. She *had* to ignore it. 'You're saying all of that combined appears to outsiders as if I'm a nightmare, but also that we're in love.'

'Exakt.'

His words sounded through her again—*'the feeling I have an ally. It has all been wonderful'*—and she had to take a deep breath. Was Luis's heart more invested than he realised?

That was dangerous thinking, and yet a flutter started in her belly and her hands clasped as if in prayer. Which told her that her own feelings were far more engaged than she'd ever meant for them to be.

Swallowing, she turned back on her side. 'We're no closer to working the mystery out than we ever were.'

He shrugged. 'It's Christmas, the time of miracles. I can't help feeling we'll get to the bottom of it yet. Like you said—we're smart. Not to mention determined. But today is for fun.' He glanced at his watch. 'Are you planning to ring your parents?'

She glanced at her watch too—the beautiful Rolex that made her smile whenever she looked at it. 'I rang them this morning, before I emerged from the bedroom.' To try and give herself a harsh dose of reality after that kiss, but they hadn't picked up. 'I left a message on the answering machine and texted a group Merry Christmas.' That they hadn't seen fit to respond to yet. 'It'll be midnight there now.'

They were silent for a while. She suspected Luis dozed, but her mind was too full. *You also make me happy... It has all been wonderful.* If Luis's emotions had become engaged—and she knew that was a big if—but if they had...

What?

She swallowed and stared into the fire. Maybe it was just the magic of the day. Maybe she was just caught up in the warmth and kindness of his family. Maybe...

Questions, so many questions, and she couldn't find an answer to any of them.

Ruby's phone rang not long after she'd slipped upstairs to pull on a thicker pair of socks before she and Luis launched into another session of roller skating. Her mother.

'Mum! Merry Christmas! It must be the wee small hours there.'

'Two a.m.,' her mother replied shortly. 'I couldn't sleep.'

She winced at her mother's tone. 'Did you have a nice day?'

An impatient breath sounded down the line. 'It would've been merrier if you'd been here, Ruby.'

She blinked. They missed her?

'Christa and I ran ourselves ragged in the kitchen all morning. It's why we couldn't answer your call. A little help would've been nice. I'm absolutely exhausted now. Too exhausted to sleep.'

Which was somehow Ruby's fault? The hopeful balloon inside her deflated. She waited for her mother to say something along the lines of never realising how much work Ruby did on Christmas Day, and kept right on waiting. 'It would've been merrier for you if I were there, but not merrier for me.'

'So that's how it's going to be from now on, is it? You're going to get all high and mighty now you've married your rich chap. From now on you're too important to help cook Christmas dinner?'

'That's not what I said.' She was silent for a moment. 'But you've never once acknowledged how much work I do at Christmas—that it's me running myself ragged every year so everyone else can have a nice time.'

She was tired of being a doormat. If she wanted to change her life, she had to start here. 'It was one of the ways I tried to show you all that I cared, but you've never cared back in return, never cared whether my Christmas was merry or not.'

'Lord, Ruby, you're like a broken record. Your jealousy of Christa—'

'This has nothing to do with Christa. It has to do with me no longer being the family doormat.'

'Stop being hysterical—'

'When was the last time you told me you loved me?'

An aching silence sounded.

'I said it to you before I left for my conference in Vegas.' She closed her eyes. 'When was the last time you told Dad you loved him? Or Christa?'

More silence.

'My guess is this morning.'

A sigh sounded down the line but no words.

'I was ten the last time you told me you loved me.'

'Ruby, just because I haven't said it in a long time…'

And yet she still didn't say it.

'Christa needed us more than you did,' her mother finally said.

'Me and Christa aren't ten any more, Mum. Don't you think it's time to start treating us equally?'

'How can I treat you equally when Christa brings me so much joy while you…'

The words speared into her with a ferocity that had her bending at the waist. 'While I?'

'I do love you, Ruby.'

The words didn't convince her though. They sounded like scraps you might feed a dog you pitied.

'But Christa always needed me while you…'

While I what?

'You never needed me, you see, Ruby.'

'Is that something you told yourself to allay your guilt at effectively abandoning me?' she shot back, stung.

'Ruby!'

'Oh, you clothed and fed me—did your duty—and I'm grateful for it, but I did need you, Mum, and abandoned is exactly how I felt.'

She waited for her mother to say something—*anything*—but she didn't.

Swallowing, she straightened. 'I only rang earlier to wish you all a merry Christmas. I hope you have a lovely Boxing Day. Give my best to everyone.'

Very quietly, she ended the call.

'Are you okay?'

Whirling around, she found Luis standing in the doorway, his eyes dark with concern.

She couldn't utter a single word, the lump in her throat stretching it into a painful ache.

'Ruby?'

She shook her head.

In two steps he was in front of her and pulling her into his arms. 'I'm sorry, sweetheart.'

She'd cried so much already today and she didn't want to cry any more, but she couldn't stem the storm that gripped her. He simply held her and let her cry. He didn't murmur any platitudes or try to make excuses for her family, and she appreciated it.

Finally quiet, she wrapped her arms around his waist and drank in his strength. His warmth and solidity. The feeling that when she was in his arms, nothing bad could touch her. 'I'm sorry,' she murmured.

'Don't apologise.' His arms tightened. 'You stood up for yourself. You were honest and brave. You should be proud of yourself.'

'I am.' And she realised she meant it. 'I'm through with being a doormat. They never appreciated it. But for the first time I'm starting to see that's a reflection on them, not me.' She eased away to meet his gaze. 'There's nothing wrong with me.' She *wasn't* hard to love. 'I'm not a bad person, I'm *not* a failure.'

He touched a finger to her cheek. 'You are wonderful. You deserve the world.'

She didn't want the world. She wanted him. Reaching up on tiptoe, she pressed her lips to his cheek. 'Thank you.'

'You're welcome.'

But this close to him, she felt the way his breath stuttered at the touch of her lips, and it made her daring and reckless. In just over a week, she'd be gone…

Pressing her lips to his throat, she touched her tongue to his skin. He stiffened, hands that gripped her upper arms tightened, but he didn't push her away. She trailed a path of slow, languorous kisses down across his collarbone.

'Ruby.' Her name was wrenched from the depths of his throat. 'You are feeling vulnerable and—'

Easing back, she met his gaze. 'I don't feel vulnerable, not in here.'

She pressed a hand to her chest. His gaze followed the action, his throat bobbing convulsively. 'Ruby, I...'

'I'm tired of regretting lost chances, of always toeing the line...of always doing things to make other people happy. I want to take something for me.' She took his hand and placed it over her left breast. 'And, Luis, I *want* you. Can you feel my heart pounding?' She arched into his hand. 'I've been burning for you ever since we woke up together in Vegas. And that kiss this morning...'

He swore but it sounded like an endearment, his hand shaping itself to her breast, his thumb brushing against her nipple, making her gasp.

'You make me feel good. I like who I am when I'm with you.' She moistened her lips. 'And I know how *good* you can make me feel in other ways. And *that's* what I want right now. It's Christmas, and that's my Christmas wish, and Christmas wishes are supposed to come true. I—'

She got no further. Luis's lips swooped down and he kissed her with a firm fierce thoroughness that left her breathless. Dragging his head closer, she kissed him back, wanting to climb into his skin, but he wrestled control back—firm yet gentle, teasing, nibbling, nipping until she was whimpering in his arms. Lifting her, he strode into the bedroom.

He halted before the bed. 'You're sure about this, sweet Ruby?'

She trailed her fingers down his chest. 'I've never been surer about anything.'

He lowered her down to the covers. 'Then I am going to make you feel so good, you will make the foundations of this villa tremble with the force of it.'

As he spoke, Luis peeled off the various items of Ruby's clothes, touching his lips to where the clothing had been, revelling in the feel of her skin and the taste of her—the lusciousness of her breasts…the sweet curve of her stomach—as he kissed his way lower and lower.

She writhed beneath him and he knew how much she'd hungered for him because he hungered for her in the same way. He had no intention of falling on her like a wild animal, though. He meant for her to enjoy every moment of their lovemaking. He wanted her to feel cherished and *enough*. Because she was.

Parting her thighs, he kissed her there, making her gasp and call his name. He teased and tempted and drove her towards the heights she hungered for, refusing to hurry or rush. This woman was magic and she deserved magic.

'Luis!' Her sharp voice penetrated the fog of sensuality that had enmeshed him. 'Luis!'

Lifting his head, he met her gaze. Whatever she saw there had her sucking in a breath. Dipping his head, he licked a long slow stroke along the seam of her.

Her hips lifted as if they had a mind of their own, but her hands on his shoulders tugged him upwards. 'Please,' she whispered. 'Please, I want you inside me. I want you with me.'

'But I want to feel you come. I want to taste—'

'This is *my* Christmas wish.' She glared, her breath sawing in and out. 'There'll be time for… other things later.'

Later? Had a word ever filled him with more gratitude? 'There will be a later?' His words were a growl.

'I don't go home for over a week. There's going to be *a lot* of later.'

He wanted to thrust an arm in the air in savage elation. 'When do I get my Christmas wish?'

'Whenever you want it,' she panted.

'It's going to be wicked.'

'I would expect nothing less.' She tried to drag his sweater over his head. 'You're wearing too many clothes.'

He resisted. 'You want me to take them off?'

'Please.'

When she asked like that, she could have the world. He undressed with the speed of light. When she reached out to touch him, though, he moved out of arm's length to slide on a condom. He wanted her too badly.

When he moved back over her, he touched his lips to hers. 'Tell me what you want.'

'I want you inside me.'

He touched fingers to curls damp with need.

She gave a funny little sob. 'Please, Luis, please. No more teasing.'

With a long slow stroke, he entered her and had to grit his teeth at the way her muscles clenched around him. He enjoyed sex, and he enjoyed making his partners come, but the way Ruby's body arched up to meet his, the moan she made and the glazed expression in her eyes made him feel virile in a way he never had before.

And then they were moving together and it was as if this were a dance only the two of them knew. When she cried out his name, her legs wrapping around his waist, her fingers digging into his buttocks to pull him as close as she could as her release shook her, he could no longer hold back. He gave her everything he had, his cries of release joining hers.

Luis woke to find Ruby trying to gently ease out from under his arm and leg without waking him.

Pulling her back, he pressed a kiss to her neck. 'Where do you think you're going?'

Turning, she traced a finger down his cheek. 'I didn't mean to wake you.'

Something in her tone, though, had his senses going on high alert. 'Are you okay?'

'Of course.'

He didn't want to ask, but he forced the words from his throat. 'Are you regretting what just happened?'

'No!'

The truth was in her eyes, but then her gaze slid away and a giant hand tightened about his chest, squeezing the air from his body.

'That was just so…*intense*. I feel…'

'What do you feel?' he managed through clenched teeth when she didn't continue.

'I don't know. Shocked. Gob-smacked.' Her lips lifted. 'Replete.'

He let out a slow breath. Those were things he could deal with. They weren't regret, heartbreak… or a yearning for something more, something he could never give.

'Perhaps if we do it again, it won't be so shocking.' He stroked a finger down her spine. 'Perhaps it will come to feel ordinary and run-of-the-mill.'

'Making love with you, Luis, will *never* feel run-of-the-mill.' Her eyes danced. 'But I'm willing to give it a go if you are—in the interests of creating some kind of immunity, you understand?'

He barked out a laugh, but then she rolled him over and straddled him. He let her take the lead, content to let her direct the course of their love-making—but this woman had tips and tricks that had his body shuddering and his limbs trembling and left him totally undone. 'Ruby,' he growled, 'if you do not—'

She sheathed him with a condom and lowered herself over him, and the breath hissed from his lungs. She held still for several long moments, as if fixing the feeling in her mind, before her hips started to move, scattering his thoughts to the four winds. Somewhere in the back of his mind he silently agreed with her—their lovemaking was overwhelmingly intense.

They'd been holding back for so long it only made sense that it would be fierce and greedy now. But that was as far as conscious thought took him before he hurtled towards oblivion and sensation and a world of pleasure.

It wasn't until they were enjoying a very lazy dinner of leftovers that Luis's haze of well-being started to lift. He couldn't wait to get Ruby back to their room to claim *his* Christmas wish, but, unbidden, her words in Vegas returned to plague him.

He shifted on his seat and his mother glanced across. 'Is everything all right, Luis?'

He forced himself to stop fidgeting. 'All of that roller skating… I used muscles I forgot about.'

That made them all laugh.

He glanced at Ruby, who looked the epitome of Christmas in a red sweater dress. *Verdammt*. Like a gift waiting to be unwrapped! He ached to unwrap her, but... She did know that nothing had changed? That this thing between them was still temporary?

Closing his eyes, he concentrated on his breathing. Earlier she'd said she was here for just over a week more. That meant she knew this was temporary. She wanted to enjoy herself, wanted to stop denying herself the things that would give her pleasure. He was totally onboard with that.

Yet... In Vegas she'd said she wasn't the kind of woman who could keep her emotions uninvolved. She'd said that she liked him and that meant her heart could be in trouble if they continued their physical relationship. His chest cramped. If that were true—

He started at a sharp contact beneath the table. Ruby had kicked him! He glared.

She shrugged. 'You were a million miles away.'

They were all staring at him and he suddenly realised he'd lost the thread of the conversation. 'Sorry. It's been a fabulous day, but it's catching up with me. So...what were we talking about?'

Ruby caught up to him by the Christmas tree, pulling him to a halt before they joined his parents in the blue drawing room. 'Are *you* regretting what happened earlier?'

He loved how she cut to the chase. 'No. I just…'

Hazel eyes raked his face. 'You're worried you took advantage of me.' She clapped her hands over her mouth as if to strangle laughter. Pulling them away, she raised a deliberately lascivious eyebrow. 'We both know the real question is… did I take advantage of you?'

'Me?' He choked back a laugh, her humour easing his mind. Throwing an arm across her shoulders, he walked her into the drawing room. 'Up for a game of Scrabble?'

'Always.'

'The two of you look so happy,' his mother said, glancing up from her seat by the fire. 'Hasn't it been a lovely Christmas?'

'Perfect,' Walter said.

'Magic,' said Luis.

Ruby nodded. 'The best.'

Something inside him solidified. The day wasn't over yet, and he intended to make it even more memorable before they fell asleep tonight.

'Have you decided what direction you're planning to take with your career yet, Ruby?'

It was Boxing Day and Luis and Ruby had decided to go sledding. They were setting up for their first run when Luis asked his question.

Ruby turned, her cheeks and nose pink with the

cold, her eyes bright. She looked utterly adorable. Considering how little sleep they'd both managed the previous night, her eyes should look as if they were hanging out of her head.

They should both *be* exhausted, even if they didn't look it. But Luis felt fired with an energy that made him feel invincible. And from the grin on her face, Ruby did too.

She sat on her sled. 'I've considered a few different options.'

'Like?'

'Working for Legal Aid—representing people who can't afford legal advice.'

'Nice idea.' He straddled his sled. 'But I imagine that could be tough. I'm getting images of overworked lawyers and meagre resources here.'

Wrinkling her nose, she pushed off. He counted to three before following. When they reached the bottom of the hill, she lifted her arms in the air and gave a whoop. 'It's like flying, isn't it? *So much fun.*'

Actually, it was Ruby who was fun. Her delight added to his own enjoyment. 'What else?' he asked as they trudged back up the slope.

'What else what?' She glanced at him. 'Oh, you're still talking about my career. Well, I could work for a firm that has a more altruistic outlook than my current firm. You know, one that does pro bono work.'

'Okay.'

'By the way, Howard and Hugh offered me the partnership on Christmas Eve. I forgot to mention it.'

He gaped at her.

She wrinkled her nose apologetically. 'We both know I'm not going to accept it, so it was a bit of an anticlimax if I'm honest. But I am beginning to like the idea of working for a charity more and more, although I don't know which one yet. And, obviously, it'll be dependent on who's hiring.'

He did what he could to appear casual. 'The family company runs a charity arm. We'd be delighted to have you join us.'

She halted. 'Luis, I—'

'I'm just throwing it into the mix,' he rushed on. 'Have you considered the UN?'

'Are you trying to get me to stay in Switzerland?'

He shrugged. 'Why not? You want to start again, don't you? Why not start again here? We could hold off on the divorce until you gained legal residency.'

'Why would you do that?'

He gave up all appearance of nonchalance. 'Because you've become important to me. You've become a dear friend. I would like you to stay.'

Behind the hazel of her eyes, he sensed her mind racing. Their gazes caught and held.

'So…?' he said when she remained silent. 'What do you think?'

She moistened her lips. 'I think I want to take you back to the villa and get you naked again.'

He went hard, just like that.

'I'm not going to,' she added.

'Why not?' Was that a *whine* in his voice?

'Because you'll get sick of me.'

That sure as heck wasn't going to happen today, but before he could say as much she added, 'And because we need to give your parents plenty of opportunity to...'

'To...?'

'I don't know—talk to us, expose themselves... do something that will help us get to the bottom of whatever it is that's going on.'

He bit back something rude and succinct.

'The job,' he finally bit out. 'What do you think about finding a job here in Switzerland, and maybe even working for Keller Enterprises?'

Hooded eyes glanced up. 'I'll think about it.'

He couldn't explain why, but the answer didn't satisfy him. It didn't satisfy him at all.

CHAPTER TEN

'RUBY, COULD I have a word?'

Ruby turned to find Claudia entering the kitchen behind her. Lunch had been three hours ago, and Luis had crashed out after… Oh, God, after yet another ridiculously *intense* session of lovemaking, but sleep had eluded her.

Her mind was like a children's jumping castle, with Luis's earlier words bouncing around non-stop.

'I would like you to stay.'

'You've become important to me.'

She was *important* to him. Her heart pounded. *How* important?

It had to mean he cared, didn't it? It had to mean he was developing feelings for her? She shouldn't get her hopes up, but she couldn't help it.

'Ruby?'

She crashed back. 'Sorry! Feeling a bit caffeine deficient.'

'Then let's get coffee and take it into the library.'

The library was another extraordinary room—

walls lined with books and with a view towards the orchard that was currently snow-covered and glistening. She'd had no idea that snow could be so *beautiful*.

'Did you have a nice day yesterday, my dear?'

Dragging her gaze from the view, Ruby took a seat and watched the older woman pour two coffees from the pot they'd carried through from the kitchen. 'I had a wonderful day,' she said, proud that her hand didn't shake as she poured milk into her mug, things inside her drawing tight.

This upcoming conversation might provide her with a clue as to what was going on with Luis's mother. She pulled in a breath and let it out slowly. *Focus.* She couldn't let Luis down.

'And you?' She kept her voice steady. 'Did you have a nice day?'

'I did. It was wonderful to see you enjoy yourself so much. It was important to Walter and I that you enjoy your first Christmas at the villa.'

'Why?' She asked the question gently. Instinct told her to act neither haughty nor entitled…or stupid.

'Many reasons.'

She sipped her coffee—delicious—and let the silence lengthen.

'First of all, you make our son very happy, and that means a lot to us.'

Her chest cramped. It was a lie, but maybe…

She and Luis cared about the same things, they

looked out for each other, and there was no denying their compatibility in the bedroom. Was it really too much to hope…?

She cut the thought off. It was dangerous to hope, and yet she found she was powerless to do anything else.

'And secondly, I have a very great favour to ask of you.'

Her heart pounded. 'A favour?' Was she about to discover the key to everything?

Walking across to a concealed wall safe, Claudia opened it and returned with several parcels wrapped in velvet. 'These jewels have been in the family for a long time. These emeralds first came into the family in the seventeenth century and were reset in the eighteen eighties by a then world-renowned jeweller. They're unique…and priceless.'

She didn't reach out a hand to touch them. They frightened her too much. 'They're extraordinary.'

'This sweet set was created by Cartier at the turn of the century.' She unwrapped a necklace, earrings and a bracelet.'

She gulped. 'Are they…?'

'Diamonds? Yes. What is your favourite gemstone, Ruby?'

Garnets were her favourites. They weren't particularly expensive, though, and she doubted they'd measure up to whatever point Claudia was building to. 'I, uh…' Her mind went blank. 'Why limit yourself to one?' She shrugged and hoped it looked confident. 'I love them all.'

'Favourite colour, then?'

'Purple.' She picked it at random. It wasn't her favourite colour. Blue—the same blue as Luis's eyes—was her favourite, but she chose a fake favourite because she was playing a role, and she was having enough trouble keeping herself grounded in this bizarre reality as it was. And what the heck, she liked purple too.

Slipping back to the safe, Claudia returned with another package, which, when unwrapped, revealed another gemstone. This one a large purple pendant.

Her breath eased and she reached out to pick it up. 'It's the most glorious colour. An amethyst?'

'A very rare sapphire.'

Very carefully she set it back to the coffee table. *Breathe. In, out. In, out.*

Claudia didn't speak. Instead, her gaze roved over Ruby's face, something vulnerable in the lines that fanned out from her eyes. Ruby swallowed and searched for something to say. 'All of these jewels, it's an extraordinary legacy.'

'Ruby, I will give these jewels to you.'

Holy crap! What?

Claudia smiled briefly. 'Yes, it is a generous gift, I know.'

She didn't want the jewels! But she bit the words back. Claudia thought her a greedy, grasping woman who'd do anything to own jewels like these. She had to maintain the charade. She nodded at the dragon's hoard on the table. 'I'd love these to be mine. What's the favour you mentioned?'

Claudia pulled herself into regal lines. 'I want you to give me grandchildren, Ruby.'

Her heart gave a giant kick. 'Luis doesn't want children.'

'I think you could change his mind.'

It took several moments before she was certain her voice would work. 'I see.'

Claudia's brow pleated. 'I thought you'd be more excited. I want to assure you that I'd have these transferred into your name—they would be yours whatever the future might hold.'

Bad Ruby would jump at the bribe Claudia was offering, but she needed to be smart about this if she wanted to find out what was really going on. Leaning towards Claudia, she asked the question burning through her. 'Why?'

The older woman blinked.

'Why is it so important to you to have grandchildren *now*? Luis told me you've never betrayed a longing for grandchildren before. He told me that you and Walter have supported his every decision—careful, for example, not to pressure him to join the family business. He said you wanted him to follow his own dreams.'

The words throbbed in the spaces between them.

'Do you know how much that meant to him?'

Claudia's gaze abruptly dropped.

'And then this year, seemingly out of the blue, it was suddenly vital he marry and settle down. No explanations, though. Just all of this pressing urgency. Your insistence took him off guard. You told him he owed you and his father. It shook him up.' She paused. 'It might also be true that I recognised that and took advantage of it.'

A swift intake of breath was her only reply.

'He loves you and Walter. He wants to make you happy. But must he do that at the expense of his own happiness?'

Claudia's face twisted and she stabbed a finger to the table. 'Luis would never regret having children. I know my son better than you, and I know *that* in the deepest part of my heart. He would be a wonderful father.'

'I agree.'

Claudia blinked.

'But you still haven't told me why it's so important to have grandchildren *now*.'

They stared at each other across the invisible divide, and Ruby held her breath.

'If I confided a secret to you, Ruby, would you promise to tell no one?'

Her chest clenched. 'Not even Luis?'

'Especially not Luis.'

If she said yes, she'd have the answer!

But even as hope lifted through her, her heart

sank. How could she betray a confidence of this magnitude? Because she could tell it was big.

Your whole reason for being here is a lie. What's one more?

Even as she tried to justify it, she found herself shaking her head. She couldn't do it. It was one lie too many. Staring at the jewels spread out like thirty pieces of silver, she let out a breath. 'I won't lie to Luis.'

'Very well,' Claudia said. 'But will you still do me this favour? The reward—' she gestured at the gems '—is large.'

'I'll consider it,' was the best she could come up with.

'Then I suggest you don't wait too long, as this offer is not indefinite.'

Without another word, Claudia rose, replaced the valuables in the safe and left.

Ruby downed the rest of her lukewarm coffee in one gulp before setting off to find Luis.

'She did *what*?' Luis stared at her as if he hadn't heard her right. 'She offered you *a bribe*?'

'An inducement to do her a favour,' she corrected. It sounded better than bribe.

'I'm going to confront her.'

He started for the door, but she intercepted him. 'And what are you going to do if she denies it? What are you going to do if she refuses to talk to you about it?'

With a groan, he wheeled back to collapse on the sofa.

Biting her lip, she lowered herself down beside him, rubbed a hand across her chest.

He glanced at that hand and then at her face and his eyes narrowed. 'What?'

She didn't want to give voice to her suspicions, but…

'Ruby, tell me what's on your mind.'

Gone was the generous and big-hearted man she knew—and quite possibly loved, though she refused to acknowledge that out loud. In his stead was a hard, unsmiling stranger.

'If you know something…'

A *determined* stranger. 'I don't *know* anything.'

'Then what do you *suspect*?'

Her heart pounded. She didn't want to give voice to her suspicions, but keeping them to herself would do no one any good. 'Is your mother in good health?'

He paled, muttered something in his native tongue she didn't understand.

'I've no proof she's unwell,' she added in a rush. 'I'm simply searching for an explanation.'

'I asked her before I left for Vegas. I thought it might explain…'

She nodded, the expression on his face making her wince.

'I was certain she wasn't lying when she said she was in the best of health.' His face twisted.

'For heaven's sake, Ruby, she's still young. And I'm sure she would have mentioned if my father were ill.'

'I know.' She didn't point out that even young people could become seriously ill. She didn't have to. This was his much-loved mother. He wouldn't want to believe for a single moment that she was sick.

Swallowing, he nodded. 'I will talk to my father. If she's unwell, he will know.'

Two nights later at the evening meal, Luis was no closer to the truth, and the ball of frustration that lodged in his chest mushroomed. Walter had assured him the previous day that Claudia was in excellent health—had even sworn it when Luis demanded it of him. While Claudia had taken to avoiding him.

He glanced across at her now. 'You've been busy, Mutti.' He cut into his schnitzel. 'I've barely clapped eyes on you for the past two days.'

She waved that away. 'There were things I needed to take care of. Speaking of which, I want you and Ruby to choose a date for a party. We might not have had a wedding for everyone to attend, but it doesn't mean we can't celebrate—'

'I see no need for that,' Ruby broke in.

She'd been remarkably quiet over the last couple of days, but he recognised the martial light in her eyes now and it fired something inside him. She was right. They needed to goad his parents until they snapped. He gave an exaggerated shrug. 'If Ruby doesn't want a party, I don't either.'

'Luis,' Walter inserted smoothly, 'it would be in the best interests of the business if you were to introduce your new wife to everyone. People will be happy for you. It would be mean-spirited to deprive them of that.'

His mother had been treating him as if he were a spoiled recalcitrant child. Why not act the part? 'I'm only interested in my and Ruby's best interests. Not the wider world.'

'Luis!' his mother admonished.

Ruby's gaze lowered to her food, but he'd seen the startled laughter in her eyes and it helped buoy him. This situation was ridiculous. But he could see the humour in it too.

'On a different topic—' Walter's voice remained unruffled '—Hans called again about playing hockey next year.'

Ruby shook her head. 'There's nothing to talk about on that subject either. But you probably ought to text him, babe, tell him you won't be playing.'

He patted her hand. 'I will, my little *Zaubermaus*. Tomorrow.'

Silence descended for several long minutes.

'Ruby,' Walter said, 'Luis tells me you're considering coming to work for the family business.'

She hid her surprise, but Luis sensed it. Had she not expected him to raise the topic with his father?

'It's a possibility. If the package I'm offered is good enough.'

'We will make it good enough,' Luis promised, plastering on the goofiest of grins. He could practically hear his mother's teeth grind together.

'Have you given it real thought, though, my dear?' Walter asked. 'It can be difficult for a young couple to, not only live together, but work together too.'

Ruby glanced up, blinked. 'Is that why you and Claudia divorced?'

Luis suppressed a wince, hardening his heart. His parents' relationship was their own affair, and none of his business. But they were all adults, and it occurred to him now that he didn't have to treat the topic with kid gloves any more. They'd all moved on from those dark traumatic days. 'That, my little *Zaubermaus*, is one of those off-limits topics.'

'Enough,' Walter said with an edge to his voice.

'Oh, well.' Ruby shrugged and turned back to the older couple with studied insolence. 'If it *is* the reason, well… Luis and I are in love. We're not going to make the same mistakes you two did.'

Walter gasped, unable to hide his shock. One look at his face had Claudia shooting to her feet.

'Don't be so disrespectful, you dreadful girl! You've no right to speak to Walter like that.'

Luis found himself on his feet then too. 'Disrespectful?' he roared. 'What's respectful about offering Ruby a bribe to have children?'

His words rang through the air, hanging over all of them.

'Oh, Claudia, you didn't.' Walter groaned and before their eyes seemed to suddenly age.

Dropping to her knees before him, Claudia took his hands. 'Don't look at me like that, Walter. He will find out eventually that you're—'

Sobs swallowed the rest of her words, and the truth hit Luis like a hard blow, making him stagger. 'Vati?'

Walter glanced up with shadowed eyes.

The ground beneath his feet refused to right itself and Luis grabbed the back of a chair to keep himself upright. 'It is *you* who is ill.'

How could he have been so blind? So stupid?

Walter dragged a hand down his face before giving a heavy nod. 'I wanted to protect you, Luis. I did not wish to worry you until I knew myself the full extent of my condition. I knew you would feel pressured to take over the reins of the company earlier than planned. The expansion of your division is going so well, I did not wish to interfere with that.'

'How ill are you?'

The older man was silent for several long moments. 'I have been diagnosed with Parkinson's disease.'

The words echoed in the sudden silence. Luis's heart pounded so hard against his ribs he could hardly breathe.

'I'm sorry I did not tell you sooner, son.' He brushed a hand across his eyes, one arm firmly around Claudia. 'If I am being honest, I did not wish to acknowledge my own mortality. I wanted time to absorb the news for myself.' He blew out a long breath. 'I wanted to get my consternation… my fear, under control first. I did not want to have to ask for help. Stupid pride, I know, but…' He trailed off.

He hadn't wanted to be a burden.

'I found out by accident.' Claudia wiped her eyes and rose to her feet, clasping Walter's hand in both of hers. 'And your father swore me to secrecy.'

'How ill are you, Vati? What is being done?' And what, as a family, could they do to help?

He listened as his father outlined his treatment, the drugs he was taking, and the doctor's prognosis. It was entirely possible that he could lead a healthy, active life for many years yet to come.

That news had some of the tension in his shoulders easing. New research was being carried out; new discoveries made every day. His father had the very best medical advice on offer. They would do everything they could to slow the progression of the disease.

Walter touched on several thoughts he'd had concerning Keller Enterprises' future—different options for CEOs and the company's direction. Claudia proclaimed herself happy to be CEO for the next five years.

'I will do everything I can to help.' Luis sat and took his father's hand. 'I know in all likelihood you have many years left to you, but you must make a bucket list—a list of all the things you have wanted to do or meant to do, but have never found the time for or have kept putting off. You have worked hard all of your life, Vati. It is now time for you. We must make the time you have left the best.'

He did not want to think of a world without his father in it. He'd always expected that to be a long way in the future. And it still might be.

But it might not either.

Forcing his head up, he met his mother's eyes. 'This is why you wanted me to marry?'

Her shoulders sagged. 'I should've been more specific. I wanted you to marry *and* have children. Your father always wanted more children and it was something I couldn't give him. I knew, though, that grandchildren would gladden his heart.' She bit her lip. 'I have felt so *powerless*. But I thought that's something I could help bring about.'

He could see how much his father's illness had

rocked her. She'd needed an outlet, something to fixate on.

'I wanted—needed—to do something that would make a difference. Children are such a joy, Luis, and feel...like having them in his life would be propitious.' She swallowed. 'I thought it would bring Walter some peace.'

All the reasons behind her relentless badgering and the stern lectures she'd inflicted on him now made sense.

'*That's* why you wanted Luis to marry?' Walter stared at Claudia. 'I thought it was because my illness had forced you to confront your own mortality, making you clucky for a new generation. I wanted you to have that before I was gone. I knew it would be a comfort to you.'

Luis rubbed a hand over his face. They'd both been trying to give the other what they thought they'd most wanted. In different circumstances he might laugh.

'But, Claudia,' Walter said, 'you descended to *bribing* Ruby?'

Claudia swallowed and nodded. 'I know. It was unforgivable.'

'Nonsense.' Ruby shook her head. 'You lost perspective, that's all. She's been worried and grieving for you, Walter.'

They all stared at her in astonishment.

'Also—' she folded her arms '—when are the two of you going to stop being such nincompoops?

It's as clear as day that the two of you still love each other. And I'm not talking about *as best friends*. Don't you think it's time to be honest with each other?'

Claudia gave a funny little hiccup. 'I'm afraid you're mistaken, my dear. Walter—'

'She's not mistaken about my feelings, Claudia, my love.'

Claudia swung to Walter, her face transforming. Luis gaped. But…

A warm, firm hand wrapped around his arm and led him away.

The full story emerged at breakfast the next morning. Seventeen years ago, after years of trying to have another baby, his mother had discovered she could no longer have children. Knowing how much Walter wanted a large family, she'd initiated the divorce without telling him why. She'd known what a decent man he was and knew he'd stick by her, but feared it would be at the expense of his own happiness. She'd hoped he'd marry again and have a brood of children.

Walter, in his turn, hadn't contested the divorce, even though Claudia was the only woman he'd ever loved, because he'd thought she needed to be free. Instead of setting out to woo her again, he'd set out to become her best friend so that she would always be in his life.

As soon as she'd discovered that Walter had

Parkinson's disease, Claudia had panicked. Where were all the children he was supposed to be surrounded with? That was when she'd begun hounding Luis to marry, to settle down. She'd wanted him to provide the children she'd been incapable of.

'I'm sorry, Luis. It wasn't fair—'

'It's okay, Mutti. I understand.'

But he didn't. Not really.

She then took Ruby's hand. 'My dear, I'm truly sorry for what took place in the library yesterday.'

Ruby's lips curved upwards, making heat pool in his loins. 'Consider it forgotten.'

'You coming here has been the most...unexpected of blessings,' Claudia said.

After Walter and Claudia had retired for *privacy*, Luis swung to Ruby. 'Can you believe that?'

Her gaze raked his face, and one shoulder lifted in a careful shrug.

He stabbed a finger in the air. 'This is what believing in love does!'

She huffed out a laugh and folded her arms. 'This should be good.'

He ignored her sarcasm. 'My parents are now not only going to risk their friendship, which they fought so hard for, but they're now going to risk their peace and happiness too!'

She blinked.

'Once again they believe themselves madly in love, but what's going to happen when it lets them down? As it inevitably will.' He slashed an arm through the air, pacing down the length of the dining room and back again. 'How can they be so stupid? So...*irresponsible*?'

Would he once again have to witness the trauma and pain they'd suffered seventeen years ago? Would he again have to help them pick up the pieces and find the strength to carry on? His hands clenched so hard he started to shake.

'You would have them deny their love for each other? Just to keep you feeling safe and comfortable?'

Love? *Ha!* 'Why can't they see love for the lie it is? If they were honest with themselves—'

'No!' And suddenly Ruby was in his face, eyes flashing. 'If they'd been honest with each other seventeen years ago, they'd have never been in this mess in the first place. If Claudia hadn't lied about her reasons for wanting the divorce, if Walter hadn't so easily agreed to said divorce...if they'd told the other how they'd really felt, *then* the divorce would never have happened and you wouldn't be railing against love in this ridiculous fashion!'

She looked magnificent. 'You're never going to convince me, you know.' He didn't know why he was goading her. Except he loved the colour in her cheeks and the way her eyes flashed and the energy that crackled from her.

'You can take your contentment, Luis, and...

do something rude with it! Joy will trump your tepid contentment. Every. Single. Time.'

She punctuated those last three words with a firm finger in his chest. He couldn't resist any longer, his lips swooped down to capture hers in a fiercely wild kiss. She kissed him back with an abandon that made his knees tremble, her fingers tangling in his hair. Backing her up against a wall, he lifted her up and she wrapped her legs around his waist.

'Someone will see,' she said, tearing her mouth from his.

Reaching blindly to his left, he opened the door to a storage room, slammed it behind them, his lips ravishing her throat and along her collarbone. The buttons on his shirt popped as she clawed her way beneath it. Seeking hands touched burning flesh and he sucked in a breath. She made him feel alive. On fire and alive, and he wanted to lose himself to the sensation.

Ruby glanced up when Luis entered their sitting room bearing a tray—the tea he'd promised her after...

She didn't know what to call what had just happened in that storage room. Their lovemaking had taken on an edge—something needy and fierce that had rocked her to the core. A part of her argued that it had to mean something—that Luis's feelings for her were growing. And yet his continual insistence that romantic love was a myth kept circling in her mind. Surely what had just happened between his parents proved that love wasn't a lie?

Focus on the here and now.

'I'm sorry about your dad.'

He collapsed to the sofa beside her, dragged a hand down his face.

Rising, she poured the tea, pushed a mug into his hands. 'He's been diagnosed early and the drugs will slow the progression of the disease. He could live a full and healthy life for many years yet, don't forget that.'

'I know. It's just…'

'You love him and can't help worrying about him.' She settled back beside him. 'But at least now you've uncovered the mystery. That's something to feel grateful for.'

He nodded.

'And we can dispense with the charade now too.' Which, as far as she was concerned, couldn't come soon enough.

He set his mug on the coffee table. 'Let's not do that just yet. Let's give them a chance to catch their breath. They've a lot on their minds.'

She stilled. And then her heart gave a giant kick. He didn't want the charade to end? That had to be a good sign, didn't it?

'You've another week before you return to Australia.' His lips lifted. 'And I still want to talk you into working for Keller Enterprises.'

She couldn't return his smile. The faint niggle at the back of her mind became a sudden and deep burn. She was spinning castles in the air. She was in danger of seeing only what she wanted to see instead of the truth. And the truth was that Luis didn't believe in love.

She folded her arms so he couldn't see the way her hands shook. 'You claim your parents would be happier if they were honest with themselves.'

'Yes.'

'But honesty isn't the best policy here?'

'Look, I—'

'Maybe, Luis, what you really need to do is be honest with yourself.'

'What on—?'

'I need a shower and a nap.'

Turning, she fled to the bedroom. Resting her back against the closed door, she stared sightlessly across the room. How honest was she going to be with Luis before she left? Did *she* believe honesty was the best policy? Was she going to tell him that she'd fallen in love with him? Was there even any point in confessing such a thing?

CHAPTER ELEVEN

AT BREAKFAST THE next morning, Luis's gaze turned to Ruby again and again. An ache started up behind her eyes. She'd gone into herself, as she did when she was around her parents and Christa, and she knew her distance bothered him, but couldn't he see that maintaining this charade, acting as if they were in love and married, was…?

She swallowed. Couldn't he see it was hurting her?

Did you conveniently forget he said that he wouldn't fall in love with you?

She flinched. What was that called in chess—a checkmate?

She shook her head. A checkmate was when someone won, when they defeated their opponent. She might feel defeated but it didn't feel as if anyone was winning here either.

'Vati, please help me talk Ruby into working for Keller Enterprises.'

All three heads at the table turned in her direction, watching…waiting. She couldn't muster even the smallest of smiles. 'What's it called when neither side wins at chess?'

Walter blotted his mouth with a napkin. 'Stalemate.'

'That's it! It was bugging me. All I could think of was checkmate and I knew that was wrong.'

Claudia's eyes narrowed. 'Ruby, are you okay?'

It wasn't part of the plan for her *not* to be okay. 'Perfectly, thank you.'

Walter stared at her. 'You are having second thoughts about working for Keller Enterprises?'

She shrugged. 'You made a good point the other day about how challenging it could be to live and work with your spouse.'

'But we'd be working in different sections,' Luis pointed out. 'We probably wouldn't even see each other at the office.'

She opened her mouth but he rushed on.

'And even if we did…'

She glanced up at his hesitation.

'Ruby, you're my best friend. We might have disagreements, but we can work anything out.'

Except her falling in love with him. He wouldn't be able to work that one out.

'After Luis mentioned you might be interested in working for Keller Enterprises, I researched your work history.' Walter pushed his plate away. 'I was impressed, Ruby. You clearly have an exemplary work ethic. I sincerely believe you would be an asset to the company. I hope you'll recon-sider.'

She blinked. Given all the hell she'd put him and Claudia through over the last three weeks, the fact he could still look with a kindly eye on any section of her life humbled her. 'That's very kind of you, Walter. Thank you.'

'And I—'

'But I sincerely believe it'll be for the best if I don't work for the family company.'

Luis's face twisted. 'But, Ruby—'

'You've known me for a month, Luis!' The words shot out of her with more force than nec-essary. Dragging in a breath, she tried to temper her tone. 'You claim I'm your best friend, but—' a lump stretched her throat into a painful ache '—you've known me a month. You think you know me, but maybe you don't. In another month you might decide otherwise.'

He gaped at her.

'And then I lose everything. I need to keep some-thing that's just mine.'

He paled, his mouth a tight line. 'You misjudge me.'

'Do I?'

Their gazes clashed. She watched as the frus-tration in his eyes evolved into... She frowned.

Resolution?

He swung to his parents. 'I need to tell you the truth about my and Ruby's marriage.'

Walter stilled. Claudia's eyes went wide.

Ruby stared. Did he really mean to tell them the truth?

'We woke up in Vegas married, with little recollection of the night before.'

She winced. It sounded ugly and irresponsible when put so baldly.

'Don't get me wrong, we'd had a great week together. We'd become friends. But getting married wasn't part of the plan.'

'It wasn't Luis's fault, though.' She couldn't have them thinking badly of him. 'I'd been passed over for a promotion—'

'One she'd deserved.'

'And he took me out dancing and did everything he could to cheer me up.'

'Did it work?' Claudia asked.

'Like a charm. It was one of the best nights of my life.'

Walter refolded his napkin. 'I thought you said you couldn't remember that night.'

'Well…' she glanced at Luis '…we kind of pieced it together.'

Claudia clasped her hands together and rested them on the table. 'What was your reaction when you realised you were married?'

She blinked. 'Truthfully?'

The older woman nodded.

'Initially we were horrified, but then…' How to say this without sounding dreadful?

'Hysterical laughter,' Luis finished for her. 'I'm not sure either one of us had ever found anything funnier.'

Claudia sat back with a satisfied expression on her face.

'We agreed, however, that we would have to dissolve the marriage.'

Claudia frowned.

'But then I proposed a plan to Ruby that would help us both. I wanted her to get the partnership she deserved, and once her name was linked with the Kellers, I knew it would be a sure thing.'

Walter nodded.

'While I wanted to bring home the wife from hell to…'

'Punish me,' Claudia murmured.

'There might've been an element of that.' Luis grimaced and dragged a hand through his hair. 'I'm not proud of it. But mostly I wanted an opportunity to find out what was going on. I thought being married to Ruby would help me do that, while showing you that whatever view of me and marriage you had, it was a lie. I hoped it would goad you into revealing the truth.'

Claudia dragged in a breath but nodded.

'I'm sorry for lying to you both. I was desperate to find out what the problem was and fix it. I hope you'll forgive me.'

Ruby watched in wonder as his parents nodded, Walter rising to clap him on the shoulder,

Claudia to embrace him briefly. They apologised for not taking him into their confidence too.

'So, you see, Ruby is not actually the money-hungry, controlling shrew she's been pretending to be. Before we embarked on this adventure, she insisted I sign a nuptial agreement that gave her nothing. She has continually told me that the wedding and engagement rings will be returned to me when this is all over, along with the Rolex, and the ruby necklace I gave her for Christmas. I will accept the engagement ring back as that is a part of our family's history, but she is keeping everything else.'

'No way, Luis—'

'She's warm and kind and deserves the best that life has to offer.'

All the protests died in her throat. Her eyes stung. She wanted to believe his words. She knew he meant them. But the thing she most wanted he would never give.

He turned back, spread his hands wide. 'See, Ruby? It's all out in the open now. You need have no scruples in accepting a position at Keller Enterprises.'

An ache stretched through her chest, and her temples throbbed. She had to swallow before she could speak. 'In this glorious vision you have for my future, I'm working for Keller Enterprises... Where am I living?'

'Why, here, of course! We have the room and we're practically family.'

'So we continue your family's tradition of divorced couples living together?'

'Why not? We are best friends and—'

'No, Luis, we're not!'

His head rocked back.

'You're so blind. Best friends is not...' She covered her face briefly before dragging her hands away. 'Best friends is not the way I feel about you. I know you're going to hate this, Luis, but I've fallen in love with you.'

The ground beneath Luis's feet shifted. He pushed away from the table and Ruby and the damning words she uttered. No. *No!*

When he reached the far end of the table, he spun back, thrusting a finger at her. 'That wasn't supposed to happen. You promised!'

She shot to her feet. 'I told you what would happen if we made love again.'

'You initiated it!'

'Oh, and what a fight *you* put up!'

She was right. He hadn't put up any fight at all. 'That's not what I meant. I thought...' He dragged both hands back through his hair. 'I thought it meant you'd changed your mind—that you could keep your feelings out of it.'

Her hollow laugh hurt him in places he didn't

know he had. 'That's just what you wanted to think.'

She was right. His need for her, his desire, had overshadowed all other considerations. He'd been selfish. 'Ruby, I—'

'It's what I wanted to think too. And I decided it was worth the risk.'

He closed his eyes. He'd never been worth that risk.

'I know you told me you didn't believe in love.'

His mother's gasp sounded loud in the sudden quiet of the room. He could feel both his parents' eyes burning into him, but he couldn't drag his gaze from Ruby. He had to make this right. *Somehow.*

'The problem was, Luis, you gave me reason to believe you were developing feelings for me too.'

'I do have feelings for you! Just not love.'

His father sighed, his mother's hand flew to her mouth, and Ruby flinched. He was making such a hash of this, but to lie—

Ruby strode down the length of the table to push a finger in his chest. 'You think telling yourself love doesn't exist is protecting your heart, but what it really means is that you're missing out on a full and joyful life.'

He opened his mouth, but couldn't push a single word out.

'Is all of the hard work you put into protecting your heart really worth it, Luis?'

His mind whirled, but out of all the thoughts in his head one became increasingly clear. He'd hurt her. He'd promised himself he wouldn't, but he had. What kind of friend did that make him?

'Our marriage always had an end date.' She dragged in a breath that made her entire body shudder. 'We've achieved all the things we set out to. It is better for me if this ends now.'

And then she was gone and he'd never felt more bereft in his life.

A knock had Luis swinging towards the door. It wasn't Ruby who stood there, though, but his mother.

'May I come in?'

He gestured her into his childhood bedroom, indicated the easy chair that sat at the end of his bed and closed the curtains against the dark he'd been sightlessly staring out at. That same dark pressed against his heart. 'Have you spoken to Ruby? Is she okay?'

His mother's dark eyes surveyed him as she took the seat. 'She's a lovely young woman.'

'Yes.'

'It was a dangerous game to play, Luis.'

He collapsed to the end of the bed. 'It was only supposed to be a couple of friends helping each other out.' No one was supposed to get hurt. 'And you haven't answered my question. Have you spoken to Ruby?'

'Yes.'

'And…?'

'I didn't know you don't believe in love.'

He couldn't meet her eyes. 'It has never come up in conversation between us.'

'I should have realised.'

'I don't see—'

'I should've realised that would be your reaction, the conclusion you came to, when your father and I divorced.' She shook her head. 'You worried so for us. You worked so hard to smooth everything over and to look after us. I'm sorry you felt such a responsibility. We shouldn't have allowed you to shoulder so much of that.'

'You and Vati were both grieving. You've nothing to apologise for.'

'I've much to regret, but one can only turn their eyes to the future rather than the past. That is something I've learned these last few days.' She pressed her hands together. 'Luis, what you need to understand is that in many ways it is harder to witness the pain of someone you love than it is to experience that pain yourself. To feel so helpless in the face of such pain is…' She touched a hand to her chest. 'It's a terrible thing.'

What was she trying to tell him?

'You saw the worst of our pain because your father and I were trying to hide it from each other—to spare each other. It never occurred to me that you would interpret it so badly.'

'It is not that I interpreted it badly.' He spoke carefully. 'I simply decided that I never wished to feel that way myself.'

'Hence, you told yourself love was a myth and a lie. What you have never realised, though, is that I would gladly experience all of that pain again, ten times over, to spend whatever time your father and I have left together.' She leaned towards him. 'To spend just one day with him.'

His jaw dropped. 'You have forgotten—'

'I have forgotten nothing!'

She couldn't be serious! But the truth shining in her eyes told him otherwise.

'Why didn't you tell your father and me the truth about your marriage yesterday—once all the other truths had come out? Why did you want Ruby to continue with the charade?'

He rolled his shoulders again. 'I wanted to give you and Vati a chance to catch your breath. So much had changed so quickly and—'

'Or perhaps you were enjoying the charade too much to let it go.'

His mouth dried. There was truth in his mother's words. Ruby had accused him of acting as if he'd developed feelings for her. Making love with her, though, had been magic and he hadn't wanted it to end. She was right. He'd been sending her mixed messages and she'd deserved better from him.

'Is Ruby okay?'

'Oh, Luis.' His mother rose. 'Her heart is broken. What do you think?'

Swearing, he strode across to the window and flung the curtain open again, welcomed the dark that greeted him. If he could turn back the clocks and undo his actions…

But would you? a secret voice whispered. *Would you surrender the opportunity to make love with Ruby?*

The last week had felt precious. Would he give it up?

For Ruby's greater happiness? He rubbed a hand over his face and nodded. Yes. Yes, he would. But to not have those memories… What a loss that would be.

'I suspect you're going to have a sleepless night.'

He glanced around at his mother. He'd forgotten that she was still there.

'One of the things you ought to ask yourself while you're staring at the ceiling or out at the dark is—are you truly prepared to let Ruby go?'

He *had* to let her go.

'Do you honestly believe you'll be happier without her in your life?'

Claudia left and Luis turned back to the dark. Would he be happier…?

Flinging himself down on his bed, he stared at the ceiling.

Would he be happier?

It wasn't a question he was accustomed to asking himself. In the past all his focus had been on avoiding the things that he knew would make him *un*happy.

Luis didn't fall asleep until dawn had started to lighten the sky outside his window and then he slept later than he meant to. Even then it took an effort to force himself out of bed. The only thing that compelled him to throw the covers back and plant his feet on the floor was his need to speak to Ruby. He needed to find a way to make things easier for her.

Both Walter and Claudia were seated at the kitchen table when he lurched through the door. They surveyed him over steaming mugs of coffee. He pointed to the pot. 'Is that fresh?'

At his mother's nod, he grabbed a mug and filled it, taking several careful gulps. 'Have either of you seen Ruby this morning?'

'Oh!' Claudia's face fell. 'I thought when neither of you appeared at the usual time that…'

She trailed off and he tried not to wince at the hope she tried to hide.

Ursula set a plate of bacon and eggs in front of him, then hesitated. He glanced up. 'Have you seen her, Ursula?'

'Not seen, no. But…' She frowned. 'A taxi collected someone very early this morning. That's not unusual if one of you is off to the airport so I didn't think anything of it. But as you're all here…'

Luis was on his feet before she'd finished and racing to their suite. Flinging the door open, he knew immediately that the rooms were empty— empty of Ruby. On the table sat a package and a letter addressed to him. A glance at the package confirmed it contained her wedding and engagement rings, the Rolex, and the ruby pendant he'd given her for Christmas.

His fingers shook as he tore open the envelope and unfolded the single sheet inside.

Dear Luis,
I think it best if we don't put ourselves through any kind of harrowing goodbye. I suspect you're still cross with me for falling in love with you—

He wasn't cross. He was *gutted*!

—and angry with yourself for allowing it to happen. I didn't mean for it to happen and nor did you. No one is to blame, so stop beating yourself up. Also, just so you know, I will be fine. Broken hearts mend—

Perhaps, but how long did it take?

—and I have an exciting new life to look forward to.

He fell down to the sofa. This couldn't be happening. She couldn't just be gone.

Please know that the last three and a half weeks have been a dream. It was such an honour to spend Christmas with you and your family in your amazing castle.

'Villa,' he corrected under his breath.

Give my apologies to your parents for my not taking my leave of them. They were such gracious hosts in the face of our absolute awfulness. You must tell them how difficult we found it. They'll appreciate the joke.

Darkness hovered at the edge of his vision. Ruby was gone.

I would love to say let's keep in touch, but I don't believe that would be in my best interests. And from now on, Luis, I'm no longer martyring myself on the altar of other people's expectations.

That, at least, made him smile. 'Good for you, Ruby.'

I will never forget you, and I wish you every happiness in the world.

She signed it simply, *Ruby x*

'She's gone?' his mother said from behind him.

He didn't answer, just handed her the letter.

Darkness closed its jaws about him, squeezing all the light and happiness from his world. He'd lost his best friend and he didn't know if he'd ever feel happy again. She'd gone, driven away, because...

He lifted his head, something deep inside him clicking into place. His heart pounded and his head thumped. Shooting to his feet, he swung around. If he couldn't live without her then that had to mean... 'I love Ruby!'

His mother lifted her hands heavenwards. 'Finally, he sees the light!'

Walter just grinned.

He needed to move, and move fast. 'I need you to find out what flight she's on.'

'On it,' his father said.

Luis grabbed his phone charger and rifled through the documents on the table until he found his passport. 'Ring me when you find out. And book me two first-class seats on the plane.'

'Good luck,' Walter called after him.

'Drive safe,' Claudia ordered.

He made it to the airport in record time. His father rang just as he pulled into the airport car park and gave him the flight number, told him he could only book business-class seats, and said he had fifteen minutes to get to the gate.

He only made it because he had no luggage to check through.

As soon as he was in his seat, he was ordered to fasten his seat belt and the plane taxied to the runway. He had no opportunity to see Ruby prior to take-off, and he couldn't stop the impatient jig of his leg.

Only once they were in the air and the seat-belt sign was turned off did impatience give way to nerves. Would she forgive him for being so stupid? Would she forgive him for being such a coward? Gritting his teeth, he called a flight attendant over. 'This might be an unusual request, but the woman of my dreams is travelling in economy and I want to propose to her.'

The flight attendant—his name badge said Gary—stared and then straightened with a grin. 'How can I help?'

Ruby stared out of the window. *At blue sky!* How dared it be blue?

It had seemed suitably cloudy before take-off, but since piercing through the clouds the weather had become disgustingly perfect—clear blue sky, a bright yellow sun, and the clouds beneath fluffy and white. She scowled at it all.

'Ms Ruby Keller?'

Schooling her features into a mask of politeness, she turned. 'Yes?'

'I have good news,' the flight attendant said, with a disgustingly bright smile.

The only good news she wanted to hear was that Luis had miraculously realised he loved her and was on some airline phone right now begging her to return to him as soon as possible.

Ha! As if *that* were going to happen.

'Good news?' She could barely feign interest.

'You've been upgraded to business class.'

'Lucky duck,' the woman beside her said as she stood to let Ruby out of her seat.

Ruby didn't move. It took an effort to do anything. 'Why?'

The flight attendant—his name badge said Gary—glanced at a note in his hand. 'I believe your employer has upgraded you.'

How had Howard and Hugh learned which flight she was on? How had they even heard she was leaving Switzerland? For heaven's sake, she'd told them she wasn't working for the firm any more and—

'Enjoy,' said her neighbour.

She didn't want it. She needed the discomfort of the flight to distract her from Luis and the tightness that stretched her chest into a crippling ache. 'Why don't you take it? I really don't mind.'

'I'm sorry,' Gary cut in, 'but it's non-transferable.'

'Go on, love,' the woman said. 'I'm only going
to London anyway, and you've a long flight back
to Australia.'

Choking back a scream that no one deserved
because they were all being so cheerful and nice,
Ruby shuffled out of her seat and wished her
neighbour well.

Smile, shoulders back, walk tall.

She followed her mental instructions to the
letter, but inside she slumped and stomped and
howled.

'Here we are.'

Before she knew it, she was seated again and
Gary had pushed a glass of champagne into her
hand with a grin.

She gritted her teeth. It was the man's job to
be cheerful.

'Enjoy your flight.'

She sagged when he left her in peace. In her
disgustingly huge seat with a disgustingly glorious glass of champagne in her hand, and all of
that disgustingly glorious weather just outside
the window. Though, at least, this time she had
an aisle seat and couldn't actually see out of the
window.

The partition was up between her and whoever
sat on the other side, and she was aware of whoever it was moving behind it, but she was careful
not to look at them. She didn't want to encourage

conversation. She just wanted to be left alone to wallow in her misery.

Tomorrow…or maybe next week, she'd force herself to snap out of it. She had a new life to plan and she had every intention of embarking on that new life with vim and vigour.

But today all of that was beyond her.

And then the partition between the two seats slid down and something inside her snapped. 'I don't mean to sound rude—' she gulped down half her champagne before turning '—but I really don't—'

Her gaze collided with bright blue eyes. 'Luis!'

Luis was on the plane.

Luis!

What was Luis doing here?

Her thoughts jumbled, scattered…made no sense.

'Hello, Ruby.'

Her heart thumped and she had to set her champagne down before she wore it. 'What are you doing here?'

'I had to see you.'

'Didn't you get my note?'

Oh, God, he looked so tired. She fought the urge to reach across and smooth down hair that looked as if it hadn't been combed this morning. Seizing her champagne again, she downed it in one gulp.

Luis handed her his champagne. 'I did.'

Acid burned a hole in her stomach. She'd made

it plain that a clean break would be best for her. 'What you want is more important than what I want?'

'Never.'

The way he said it had a lump lodging in her throat. She knew he thought he was making things right, but he couldn't make them right. Until he believed in love, he would never make them right.

'When I woke up this morning and discovered you were gone, I panicked.'

Cutting remarks rose in her throat, but she didn't utter a single one. She didn't have the heart for them. The sooner this was over, the better. She'd let him draw a line, find his closure, and then they could both move on.

'Actually, if you hadn't left like you did—if I hadn't been given such a jolt—it might have taken me a lot longer to realise the truth.' As he spoke, he leaned across and placed the ruby pendant on her tray table.

She glared at him. 'What is that?'

'It's the Christmas gift I chose specifically for you. Do you wish me to return my roulette wheel?'

'Absolutely not!'

He raised an eyebrow.

Closing her eyes, she pulled in a breath. 'Very well.' Closing her fingers around the pendant, she stowed it in her handbag.

When she straightened, she found the Rolex sitting where the pendant had been. She folded her arms and glared. 'No way.'

'I do not care what you do with it, Ruby, but it was a gift.'

'It was a prop to convince your parents I was a gold-digging harpy.'

'We Swiss are very proud of our timepieces. I want you to have this as a memento of your time in Switzerland. It will serve you well all your days.'

Unlike him.

'And again, it was chosen with you specifically in mind. I pored over catalogues before I settled on the perfect watch for you. It cannot be given to anyone else. Please don't ask me to.'

Her eyes burned. She couldn't look at him.

'I do not care what you do with it—you can auction it off for charity if you want—but this watch belongs to you.'

A growl emerged from her throat. 'You have more money than sense, Luis.' She practically threw the watch into her handbag. 'I like the charity auction idea, though. So if you want to change your mind...'

'I will not change my mind.'

Holding her gaze, he pulled her wedding ring from his breast pocket and the engagement ring.

She couldn't speak. Tears blurred her eyes and her throat stretched into a painful ache. 'I can't,

Luis,' she whispered. 'I can't stand it. Please put them away. It was all a lie and...'

She broke off, gulping back a sob.

'I thought it a lie too. It's what I told myself. But when I woke up this morning and realised you'd gone, I— It felt like a part of me had died.'

She blinked hard, but the expression on his face didn't change.

'It hit me then that I couldn't live without you.'

And still his expression didn't change.

On the other side of the partition, he went down on one knee. 'Ruby, I love you.'

His eyes shone, his voice sounded strong and sure, and her heart leaped up to pound in her throat.

'I didn't know I'd been searching for you my whole life until you were no longer there. The thought of losing you tears my soul to shreds. Can you ever forgive me for being such a fool? I was a coward—telling myself love didn't exist in an effort to shore my heart up against heartbreak. But you are a woman worth risking everything for. I want to build a life with you. I want to do everything I can to make you happy.'

She couldn't utter a single word. He had to be lying. This couldn't be happening.

But sincerity shone from his eyes, his face had softened with an emotion she'd never seen there before, and this *was* happening.

'Please do me the very great honour of being

my wife and making me the happiest man in the world.'

'Yes!' And then she was in his arms and his lips were on hers and she was kissing him with all the passion in her heart. It was some time before she registered that the rest of the plane was cheering and clapping and Gary—bless him—was moving towards them with more champagne and the biggest of smiles.

When they were finally settled back in their seats, her hand clasped firmly in his, Luis slid the wedding and engagement rings back on her finger. She grinned stupidly at him. She couldn't help it. To her utter delight, he grinned just as stupidly at her.

'I love you, Ruby.'

She would never tire of hearing that. 'I love you, Luis.' She'd never tire of saying it either.

'Where shall we live? Where do you wish to live?'

'In Switzerland in your castle.'

'It's not—'

'A castle, I know. It's not fortified.'

'Do you truly wish to live there?'

'As long as your parents don't mind.'

'Mind? They'll be delighted!'

'It'll be good to be close at hand if they should ever need us.'

That earned her a kiss on each of her fingers. 'And work? Would you like to come and run Keller

Enterprises' charity arm? I will not be offended if you wish to do something else.'

'I would *love* to be a part of the family business.'

That earned her a kiss to the palm of her hand.

Heat licked along her veins, making her breathless. 'I have a question for you now.'

He was all attention in an instant. 'The answer is yes. Whatever you want, I will move heaven and earth to give you.'

'Children?' she said softly.

He stilled and then swallowed. 'Yes.'

'You can't just say that, Luis. You…'

He reached across to trace a finger along her cheek and her words stuttered to a halt. 'You have made me believe in old dreams again, sweet Ruby. To have a family with you—a family we could raise with all the warmth and love in our hearts—would be an honour. I could think of no greater gift you could give me.'

She had no words, her heart was so full.

On the overhead PA system, the pilot announced they'd be landing at Heathrow airport in twenty minutes, and that the weather was cloudy, but an umbrella unnecessary.

She laughed when Luis gaped at her. 'London? But I thought we were going to Sydney.'

'Sydney via London and Singapore.'

He stared at her for a moment and a gleam lit the blue of his eyes. 'We haven't yet had a proper honeymoon. How does a week in London followed by a week in Paris sound before we head home to Switzerland?'

Home to Switzerland.

Reaching across, she kissed him. 'It sounds perfect.'

* * * * *

If you enjoyed this story, check out these other great reads from Michelle Douglas

Cinderella's Secret Fling
Unbuttoning the Tuscan Tycoon
Reclusive Millionaire's Mistletoe Miracle
Wedding Date in Malaysia

All available now!